"TOO SMART" JONES

and the
Wilderness
Mystery

"TOO SMART" JONES

and the Wilderness Mystery

8

A GILBERT MORRIS MYSTERY

MOODY PRESS
CHICAGO

© 2000 by
GILBERT MORRIS

ISBN: 0-8024-4032-0

1 3 5 7 9 10 8 6 4 2

Printed in the United States of America

Contents

Adventure Coming Up

It was a lovely lizard!

As a matter of fact, it was the most splendid lizard that Joe Jones had ever seen!

Glancing over at his sister, Joe swiftly snatched up the lizard. It was emerald green and was more than six inches long. It wiggled in his hands and tried to get loose, but he held it firmly. Joe thought, *It's about time Too Smart Jones had a little excitement!*

He tiptoed to where Juliet was pulling up dried flowers for a Thanksgiving arrangement. Quickly he pulled back her plaid shirt collar and dropped the lizard down her back.

Juliet came to her feet with a screech. She tried to reach her back. She ran in wild circles around the yard. Finally she yanked out her shirttail. The green lizard hit the ground and scooted away, no doubt as frightened as was Too Smart Jones herself.

With eyes blazing, Juliet threw herself at Joe and began pounding on him. "I hate you, Joe Jones!" she cried. Joe was ten, one year younger than Juliet, but he was stronger. He easily held her wrist and said, "Why, Juliet, I thought you loved animals."

"I do, but that wasn't an animal! That was a lizard!"

"Well, lizards are animals." Joe smirked and dropped her wrist. He was tall and gangly and wore a gray pullover and jeans.

Juliet still looked furious. She had just had her birthday so was barely eleven years old. She had auburn hair and sparkly brown eyes that didn't sparkle right now. Ordinarily she put up with Joe's teasing. He guessed that the suddenness of having a lizard crawling down her back had angered her this time.

"You just wait, Joe!" she cried. "I'll get you for that!"

He still grinned. "You're not supposed to hold grudges. That's what Mom and Dad always tell us."

"Mom and Dad don't have to put up with you putting lizards down their backs!"

Juliet was not really upset, though she and Joe stood arguing for a time. She knew that somewhere down the line she would pull a trick on *him*.

"I'll be glad when Thanksgiving comes," he said, suddenly changing the subject. "I can taste that turkey now!"

"Still two weeks away. But it's still nice outside."

It was, indeed, very nice. The day was cool and clear. The smell of burning leaves was in the air. Juliet looked at the fluffy white clouds drifting slowly across the gray blue sky. "I like the fall," she said.

"Yeah. I like it, too." Joe pulled out his pocketknife, opened the blade, and began to throw it at the ground. He managed to bury it up to the hilt every time.

"What do you suppose they'll come up with for our homeschool project this fall?"

"Who knows? Not likely anything as good as a trip to the moon, though," he said rather gloomily. "Let's go upstairs. I want to show you what I've done on my invention."

They went into the house, a white two-story with green shutters, and up to their classroom. Since they were homeschooled, Juliet and Joe spent much of their time here. The walls were covered with maps and old projects, and the bookshelves were filled with books. The desks were not very neat, but Joe always said, "A neat desk is the sign of a lazy person. Busy people make a mess."

Throwing herself into a chair, Juliet said, "What are you inventing now?"

"I'm inventing an automatic page turner. Look at this." He held up a wire device. "See? You put these wings here inside the pages of a book, and that's attached onto this arm here. When you want to turn the page, you just pull this."

Juliet watched as he demonstrated. Then she rolled her eyes. "It would be a lot easier just to turn the page with your finger, wouldn't it?"

"That's the trouble with you, Juliet. You're too smart. You're so smart that you don't see the possibilities in great things."

"Don't call me too smart!" Juliet snapped.

Juliet had always been good at books and made the best grades in public school. The nickname Too Smart had attached itself to her. Somehow it stuck like glue, even now that she was schooled at home.

"And what are you two up to now?"

Mrs. Jones entered their classroom with a sparkle in her eye. She was a very pretty lady. She had auburn hair and brown eyes like Juliet's. Besides, she was a fine homeschool teacher.

"Joe showed me his new useless invention, Mom," Juliet announced with a grin.

Mrs. Jones watched while Joe demonstrated his automatic page turner. "Well, you stay here and work on your invention while Juliet and I go downstairs and have lunch."

"Hey, not likely!" Joe yelled.

"Somehow I thought you'd say that. You've never missed a meal in your life. You might forget everything else, but you never forget lunchtime."

"I'm a growing boy. I've got to keep my strength up."

Juliet helped prepare the tomato soup and the toasted cheese sandwiches. Then they had a good time with one another over the lunch table.

As they ate, Joe asked, "Where's Dad working this week?"

"He's putting in a new section of the state highway."

Mr. Jones was an engineer, and sometimes he had to work so far away that he could not get back home every day.

"He'll be home tonight, though."

"When I grow up I'm going to be an engineer just like he is," Joe announced.

Mrs. Jones smiled. "I think that would be wonderful, if that's what God has planned for you." She turned to Juliet and said, "And are you still going to be a detective?"

"She's going to be a detective. She's always solving mysteries—even when there aren't any mysteries." Joe took a huge bite of cheese sandwich. Then he reached for Juliet's. "If you don't want the rest of your sandwich, I'll take it."

Juliet slapped his hand. "Keep away from my food! And I am *not* always solving mysteries!"

"Sure you are." Joe drank the rest of his milk and left a mustache on his upper lip. "You're just a natural-born detective like Sherlock Holmes."

"And you look like a commercial for the milk company!"

"You two can argue someplace else. Now let's get things cleaned up, and then you're free for the rest of the afternoon."

"Sounds good to me," Joe said quickly. "You help with the dishes, Juliet. I'll go clean up our schoolroom."

Thirty minutes later the two of them shot out the front door. "How about a bike race?" Joe said.

Juliet agreed, and they walked to where their bicycles were locked up. "I'm glad we solved the case of the stolen bicycles," she said.

"Me too. But I'm going to keep mine locked up even if the thieves are in jail."

They unlocked the bikes and got on. Joe said, "I'll give you a head start."

Juliet took off, riding as fast as she could. It was hopeless, however. Joe was one of the fastest bicycle riders in Oakwood. They raced around several blocks, and then biked downtown, where they each bought an ice cream.

When they finally wheeled back into the Jones yard, Joe yelled.

"There's Delores and Samuel!" He shot into the yard and cut a wheelie, yelling, "How do you like this? Think I'll be ready for my circus act?"

Samuel Del Rio was eleven. His sister was nine. They both had black hair and dark eyes. "My grandfather used to ride a bicycle across a wire forty feet up in the air," Samuel said.

Joe shook his head. "I don't think I'd want to try that. How did he get the wheels to stay on the wire?"

"They were special wheels," Delores said. Both she and her brother were good acrobats. Their parents had been circus performers.

"What are you two doing here?" Juliet asked.

"Come on into the house," Joe said to their friends. "You'll have to excuse my sister. I'm trying to raise her right, but you know how it is with children. They're difficult sometimes."

The four went down to the game room in the basement, and for a time they played table tennis. As it happened, this was one game that Juliet could beat Joe at. She and Delores managed to beat the boys two games in a row.

"That's two games out of three. Have you had enough?" Juliet asked.

"Aw, we're just letting you win," Joe said. "I know it makes you feel good."

Samuel took the Ping-Pong ball and began to bat it up into the air. Like all good acrobats, he had very good coordination. "Have you heard about our fall project yet?"

Juliet and Joe both gaped at Samuel. "We haven't heard anything," Juliet said. "What will we be doing?"

"You haven't heard? Well—" Samuel caught the ball with his free hand "—it's gonna be just great."

"Tell us! What are we going to do?" Joe cried.

"We're going out on a wilderness trip, that's what. Way out in the middle of the woods. And we'll learn how to live off the land."

"Is that right?" Joe's eyes flashed with excitement.

"That would be really cool," Juliet said.

At that moment Mrs. Jones came down the stairs. "Now what's all the hubbub about down here?"

"Samuel says that we're going on a wilderness trip for our next school project. Are we, Mom? You never told us," Juliet said.

"That's what we've talked about. I just didn't want to get your hopes up if things didn't work out."

"Oh boy!" Juliet said. "That'll be great! When will we know for sure?"

"We'll know this evening."

The homeschooled youngsters and their parents met regularly to discuss school and to plan new activities. Juliet knew that the next Support Group meeting was scheduled for tonight.

She said excitedly, "I've got that new sleeping bag, and I've been anxious to try it out."

Then Joe said, "One thing's sure."

"What's that?" Samuel asked.

"If we're out in the woods, Too Smart Jones won't have any mysteries to solve." He tapped his sister's arm with his fist. "Poor Too Smart Jones!"

Juliet pulled his hair. "You just mind your own business, Joe Jones!"

"Ow!" he yelped.

"Camping will be fun," Delores said. "I've never been camping before."

"I'll take care of you," Joe said importantly. "I know all about the woods and wild animals and stuff."

Juliet sniffed. "You know all about all kinds of stuff! We'll wait and see what happens the first time you get chiggers!"

To the Woods

The church's small recreation hall was filled with parents and children. The Support Group mothers had prepared a potluck supper, and the smell of good food floated in the air. The women moved from table to table, setting out dishes, while the men stood in small groups talking. The boys and girls were gathered in one corner, waiting for the meal to begin.

Juliet looked around. "Everybody's here this time, Jenny. This is the biggest group we've ever had."

Jenny White, age ten, had very red hair and blue eyes. She was Juliet's closest friend. "It sure is," she said. "And look who's over there."

Juliet glanced across the room to where Billy Rollins, as usual, was talking too loudly and waving his arms around. "Looks like he's telling Ray and Helen some tall tale."

Ray and Helen were the Boyd twins.

"All right! All right, now!" Mr. Rollins said in a big voice. "Let's get this show on the road!"

Juliet's dad was standing beside Mr. Rollins. "I think you're going to have to talk louder than that," he said. Mr. Jones was a strong looking man, very tall and tanned.

"Well, see if you can do anything with them, Mark," Mr. Rollins said.

Right away, Mr. Jones said in a booming voice. "If you want anything to eat, you'd better be quiet!" Immediately, silence settled over the room. "That's one sure way to get their attention, Harold. Now, why don't you ask the blessing?"

Mr. Rollins prayed a rather long prayer, and at the "amen," Joe started for the food.

Mr. Jones put a hand on his head. "I don't know, Joe. Maybe I should make you wait at the end of the line."

"Aw, Dad!" Joe wailed. "I'm hungry!"

"You always are."

Juliet and Jenny went down the buffet line, filling their plates with all kinds of good things. They took small spoonfuls of salad, coleslaw, and green beans. There was lasagna with thick sauce and running over with cheese. There was fried chicken, potato salad, and rolls, and for dessert thick slices of double chocolate cake.

The girls got two lemonades in Styrofoam

cups and went to where long tables were set up. Soon Juliet and Jenny were joined by Melvin Gordon, whom nobody called anything but Flash. As always, Flash was in his wheel-chair.

With Flash was Chili Williams. He grinned and showed his plate. "Look what I got!"

Joe, who was already eating, said, "I don't have to look. You got chili."

"Sure did. Chili's the best thing there is."

Soon Samuel and Delores joined them, and for a time there was a great deal of laughter as they put the meal away.

"You know what I don't like about these potluck suppers?" Joe asked.

"I didn't know there was anything you didn't like about them," Flash said. "You eat every-thing that's not nailed down."

"Well, the food's OK, but we always have to help clean up afterwards."

"It won't hurt you," Chili said. "I wash dishes at my house anyway. It's my job."

"I do too," Juliet said.

"I'll be glad," Joe announced, "when we get out in the woods. No more dishes!"

"You think we're gonna eat with our hands?" Samuel said. "I'm taking a tin plate."

"You're just a sissy! We real pioneers don't need anything except a stick to roast a piece of meat on! Just think, no dish washing, no clean-ing up, and no baths."

"I can see you'll be pretty ripe by the time this is over," Flash said. He was eating a bowlful of banana pudding. "Won't be any banana pudding out there, either. I'll bet we'll be half-starved by the time we get back."

"It'll be fun, though," Juliet chimed in.

"Yeah, but there also won't be any mysteries for Too Smart Jones to solve."

"Now, don't you start, Joe!"

When everyone had finished eating, both parents and boys and girls pitched in to get the room cleaned up. Thirty minutes later the meeting was called to order by Mr. Rollins.

"Listen up now!" he began.

"Hey, Dad, where are we going?"

"Yeah!" Jack Tanner joined in. "What kind of special gear will we need?"

The room was nothing but hubbub for a while.

Juliet and Joe's parents were sitting directly behind them, and she heard her dad say, "I've never seen these kids so excited about anything."

"Neither have I," her mom replied. "Do you really think it will be safe?"

"Several fathers are taking time off to chaperone. We'll have enough chaperones."

Mr. Rollins then yelled, *"Everybody pipe down!"* He beat his fists three times on the table. Finally there was enough quiet so that he could be heard.

"Here's what we're going to do," he said importantly. "The Oakwood Support Group is sponsoring a week's outing in the wilderness—"

At this point, cheering broke out. Once again Mr. Rollins had to yell. "Will you please pipe down, or we won't go anywhere!"

When quiet returned, he cleared his throat. "Here's the plan. We'll meet at a wilderness camp. It's called Outdoor Experience. It's close to Riverton, about thirty miles from here. We'll leave on Wednesday and return the following Wednesday."

"Why can't we leave tomorrow?" Joe complained loudly.

"Because it takes preparation for a trip like this. I'm surprised you wouldn't know that, Joe."

Joe muttered, "Preparation! As long as I've got my pocketknife and my ax, I'm ready."

"*Ssh,*" Juliet said.

"Now," Mr. Rollins said, "Mr. Jones, Mr. Tanner, Mr. Gordon, Mr. Harris, and Mr. Williams have taken time off work to chaperone the group."

Another cheer went up.

Juliet saw Chili Williams in the row ahead smile up at his dad. Chili said, "Hey, Dad. I'm glad you're going."

"Me too, Son. We haven't done anything together like this in a long time."

Flash Gordon's father leaned over and said,

"Melvin, do you think it'll be all right? I mean with your wheelchair and all?"

"You just watch, Dad." Flash grinned. "You'll see!"

Mrs. Gordon said, "There won't be any sidewalks to use your wheelchair on . . ."

"Don't you worry, Mom. Mr. Jones says there are good trails—wide enough and smooth enough. And the Lord will take care of me."

Mr. Rollins talked awhile about the outing. "We're going to spend all week in the wilderness, and we're going to learn to live off the land."

"Aren't we taking any food along?" Samuel asked.

"Oh, sure. We'll take some staples," Mr. Rollins said. "But we're going to learn what plants and berries are good to eat—and how to trap squirrels and rabbits."

"What about fishing? I can always catch a fish," Flash yelled.

"Sure. Bring all the fishing tackle you can stick in your pocket. But remember, you're going to have to carry everything, so don't load yourself down."

"Is this ever going to be fun!" Juliet said. "We'll go hiking, and rock climbing, and canoeing. No telling what else."

Joe nudged her with his elbow. "Everything except solving mysteries."

* * *

It seemed to Juliet that Wednesday would never come. However, it did arrive.

It turned out that quite a few homeschoolers couldn't make the trip, but those who could go piled into cars and vans with their leaders and headed for the Outdoor Experience. They left before dawn, and by the time they got there the sun was beginning to illuminate the landscape.

Juliet climbed out of the car, looked around, and shivered. "It's *cold* out here," she said.

Jenny agreed. "I just hope we brought enough warm clothes."

Billy Rollins was sauntering by. He laughed loudly. "You girls don't have to worry."

"Why do you say that?" Juliet asked.

"Because you won't be here after tomorrow."

"What are you talking about?"

Billy was always making fun of somebody. "You won't be able to handle living in the wilderness. You got to be tough for this sort of thing."

"We will too!" Juliet protested.

"No, you won't. And you'll be a real drag on us guys."

"How will we be a drag?" Juliet could feel herself getting cross.

Some of the boys had stopped to listen,

and Billy winked at them. "I mean we'll have to go real slow because of you girls."

"You will not!" Juliet snapped.

"Will too!" Billy nodded wisely. "We'll have to baby you all the time."

"You won't have to baby us!" Delores Del Rio cried. "We can take care of ourselves!"

"Oh yeah! What about when you get scared at night and think there's a bear or a wolf or something out there?" Billy laughed. "Don't come crying to me when you get scared."

"Don't worry about that happening," Juliet said.

"And let me tell you something, Too Smart." Billy stopped grinning. "It's one thing when you got a nice, warm living room to go home to, but it's another thing out here. I'm telling you it's going to be rough, and you girls won't make it!"

Jenny pulled Juliet away. "Don't pay any attention to him! You know how he is."

"I know. But all the same, I wish he wouldn't always talk like that."

Soon the vehicles headed back to Oakwood. The chaperones organized their groups, and they started into the woods.

Chili Williams was full of vim and vigor. Right away he said, "I'm going to blaze the trail for you!" He ran ahead, and with his ax he removed a little bark from a tree. "Follow this, and you won't get lost!" he yelled.

"Can you make it, Flash?" Samuel asked.

"Sure. Not bad at all."

"It's harder without sidewalks," Juliet said with a worried expression. She had wondered how Flash and his wheelchair would get along in the woods. Thick trees lined the trail, but the path itself looked hard and smooth. "You want me to push you?"

"Push me? You just try to keep up!"

Flash never had a discouraging word to say. Juliet watched him maneuver down the woodsy trail.

"I'm the motor!" Samuel yelled once. "Here we go, Flash! Hang on!" He put his hands on the back of the wheelchair, and the two went scooting along.

"Is he going to do all right?" Daniel Saville asked. Daniel and his sister were new in Oakwood.

"Sure he is," Juliet said. "The trail's better than I thought." Then she added, "I'm Juliet Jones. We don't know each other yet, but I guess we will by the time we've spent a week in the woods."

Daniel Saville grinned down at her. "I like it in the woods," he said. "I like anything outdoors."

The boy was dressed in army fatigues and looked very fit. After a while, he ran ahead and shoved Samuel out of the way, saying, "Give your motor a break."

Flash looked around at him. "Hi. Don't think we've met."

"I'm Daniel Saville. This is my sister, Kelsey."

"Flash Gordon. But you don't have to push. I can make it."

"Aw, it'll be fun. Let's go."

The hike through the woods seemed to be fun for everyone. The sponsors made sure that no one wandered off, and Mr. Jones walked at the very end of the line, watching everybody. When Juliet dropped back to walk beside him, he said, "Lots of fun, eh?"

"Sure is, Dad. Did you do anything like this when you were a boy?"

"Yep. Been a camper all my life."

"I was a little worried about Flash," Juliet said. "But he's going to be fine."

"We chose a place with trails that are wheelchair-friendly. That boy has lots of spunk."

"He's got lots of faith too. He really believes God's going to get him out of that wheelchair someday."

"We'll just help pray that He will."

The campers made their way over little hills and down through wooded areas. They pushed Flash's wheelchair through small streams, then climbed more hills. By the time they got to their campsite, some of the youngsters were gasping. As a matter of fact, Mr. Rollins himself looked out of breath.

Juliet's dad was not even breathing hard, but of course he worked outdoors every day. "You'd better sit down, Harold," Mr. Jones told him.

"I believe I will—if you'll take over organizing things."

"Sure. You just take it easy." He pulled the heavy knapsack off his back. "Listen up, everybody!"

The youngsters all gathered around him.

He said, "We're going to get organized. First of all, everybody has to have a buddy. Just like a swimming partner. We can't have anybody getting lost. You got that straight?"

When they were all paired off, Joe announced, "We're ready, Dad. What do we do now?"

"How about you girls going off the trail *just a little* and gathering berries!"

"Ooh, that'll be fun!" Juliet said.

"And you boys—why don't you try to catch some fish in that brook?"

They spent the rest of the morning gathering food. Juliet found some wild grapes. She tasted one and said, "Oh, these are good!"

"Those are muscadines," her dad told her when she brought some in. "Best wild grape there is."

It sounded as if Joe and the other boys had a fine time, too. He'd caught the first fish, which wasn't very large. "But it was the first," he said.

"You wait! *I'm* going to catch the biggest!" Billy Rollins had bragged.

As a matter of fact, the fish were biting well, and the boys brought back quite a string.

"Look what we caught, Dad," Billy said. "And I caught the biggest one."

"Good for you."

"Now—" Juliet's dad grinned broadly "—now the fun comes."

"What's that, Mr. Jones?" Chili asked.

"I mean that it's fun to catch fish, but nobody likes to clean them."

"I don't even know how," Billy admitted.

"I do," Joe said. "I'll show you."

It was a messy, dirty job, but they got the fish cleaned. Mr. Gordon and Mr. Tanner built a fire, and soon everybody was milling around watching as the fish fried.

So the wilderness campers ate fish and grapes plus some canned beans that Mr. Jones had brought along.

"Does this ever taste good!" Juliet said.

Joe took a big bite of fish. "Things always taste better outside."

After they had eaten, he said happily, "And no dishes to wash!" They had used paper plates and had to burn them under Mr. Tanner's careful direction.

When evening came, Mr. Jones said, "Now let's tell some stories around the campfire."

It was a wonderful evening. They sang songs, they toasted marshmallows, and they listened to stories by Flash's father, who was an expert storyteller. He even knew some ghost stories.

But at last Juliet's dad said, "And that's it. Everybody hit the sack!"

Juliet went to the girls' tent and climbed into her brand-new sleeping bag. She was so tired it felt wonderful.

As a matter of fact, everyone must have been tired, for soon it was absolutely quiet except for the cry of an owl or some other night bird.

Too Smart Jones was almost asleep when she heard something.

What was that?

She had almost gone to sleep again when the sound came once more. She sat up straight in her sleeping bag and looked out the tent flap.

She saw something—she thought—but could not tell what it was. "What *is* that?" she whispered. She stared out into the gloom but could make out nothing.

Oh, it was nothing but the wind, Juliet decided. She lay down and zipped up her sleeping bag, glad that she had such a warm one. Then she thought, *It couldn't have been the wind! There isn't any wind tonight!* For a moment she felt a tingle of fear, but she whispered, "Lord, I'm not going to be afraid. Please take care of me and everybody else."

Juliet's last thought before drifting off to sleep was *I know I heard something—I just don't know what.*

Living
Off the Land

Juliet woke up with a start. She heard men's voices outside and knew that her father was already up.

"We'd better get up," Jenny said.

"I think we'd better."

Delores stirred and came out of her sleeping bag. They had all slept in their shirts and blue jeans. Looking down at herself, Delores laughed. "Look how wrinkled I am! I wouldn't go anywhere in town looking like this."

Juliet unzipped her bag and sat up. She had even left her socks on. She slipped her feet into her boots. "I wouldn't either. But out here in the woods, we can wear anything we want to."

"I wonder what we're going to have for breakfast," Jenny said next.

"Leftover fish?" Juliet guessed. "What else?"

"Ugh!" Delores said. "I think I'll do without."

Breakfast was better than that, though. Mr. Gordon had brought a lot of granola and some rolls. The youngsters made out with that and some of the berries that Juliet and the other girls had picked the day before.

"I'm glad we don't have to scrape around to find something to eat when we're at home," Joe mumbled as he gobbled the last of his grapes.

"It'll make you appreciate my cooking more when we do get home," Juliet said.

"I'd appreciate it right now," Samuel said. "What wouldn't I give for some scrambled eggs and bacon!"

"Don't even talk about it," Jack Tanner was a tall, thin boy with light brown hair. He was Jenny's stepbrother. "I'd like to be sitting down right now at a Waffle House."

Billy Rollins grumbled, "Yeah, or anywhere else."

Juliet giggled. "I thought we were going to have to keep up with you boys. You see how that went."

"You just wait," Billy said. "You'll find out. This is just the second day. You won't last more than three days!"

Billy headed toward the boys' tent then, and Juliet and the others began talking about what they were going to do that day.

"Hey, what's going on here?"

Juliet looked over to where Billy stood by the tent, searching through his gear.

"What's the matter, Billy?" Samuel asked. "Did you lose your Snickers bars?"

"No! I've lost my compass!"

Joe ambled over and looked at the pile of stuff that Billy had brought along. "I don't see how you can tell if anything's missing in that mess."

"*You* probably took it! That's probably where it went!" Billy said.

"You're always ready to blame somebody else! Why don't you blame yourself?" Joe asked.

"I didn't lose that compass. Somebody took it!"

At that moment Mr. Rollins came along. "What's the matter, Billy?"

"Somebody took my compass!"

"Oh, surely not! You just misplaced it."

"Maybe you didn't even remember to bring it," Samuel said.

"Didn't bring it? Do you think I'm an idiot, going out in the woods without a compass?"

"Well, don't worry about it. I'll get you another one when we get back home," Mr. Rollins said, walking on. "And a much better one."

Juliet whispered, "Mr. Rollins always says that. Anytime Billy has a problem, he thinks he can solve it by buying him something."

Billy noticed the girls whispering and glared at them. "I'll get you guys! I know one of you took my compass! You just wait!"

The group divided up then and got ready to take the trail into the deep woods. As she put her jacket on, Juliet thought again of the rustling that she had heard last night. *Could that have been someone taking Billy's compass?* she thought. *No, Billy probably hid the compass himself just to get some attention.*

And then Too Smart Jones put the whole thing out of her mind. She knew it was going to be an active day. She didn't have time to worry about little things like Billy Rollins's compass.

Mr. Jones said. "Chili, do you think you can lead the way today?"

"You bet! I've got a trail map, and I'm the world's greatest map reader! Now if I just had a bowl of chili, I could do even better."

"I don't think you're going to find any chili out here, but let's see what you can do."

Juliet could tell that her dad liked Chili Williams very much.

"Take us out, Chili. Don't get us lost, though."

"I've never been lost once in my whole life," Chili bragged. "Stick close to me, you guys. I will take you through."

As they started off, Juliet heard her dad say to Chili's father, "That's a bright boy you've got there."

"Thank you. And those are two bright kids you've got, too." Mr. Williams was a big, strong man. He was a bricklayer and a deacon in his church too. "It's wonderful to get out into God's world and spend a little time with my boy and all these other youngsters."

"We ought to do it more often."

And so Chili led the campers through the woods.

During one of their breaks, Flash said, "Let's have a game."

"What kind of game?" Chili asked.

"A ball game."

"Don't have any balls," Chili protested. "You got to have a ball to have a ball game."

"We can find something," Flash said. He rolled his wheelchair around, looking this way and that. "What about one of these?" He leaned out of the chair and picked up a pine cone. "It's not near as big as a football, but it's bigger than a baseball."

"Then we can play pine cone football," Chili said.

"Never heard of pine cone football," Jack said. "How do you play?"

"We can make up the rules as we go along," Flash announced. "First we divide up sides. I'll have one team, and you can take the other one, Joe."

In minutes, all the youngsters were play-ing pine cone football. They broke down laughing frequently, because Flash changed the rules every few minutes. The cone didn't weigh much, and one rule was that you had

35

to hit somebody with it. Since Flash had the strongest arms, he never missed.

"Ow!" Juliet said when the scratchy cone got caught in her hair. But she pulled it off, laughing. "I'll get you for that, Flash Gordon!" She threw the cone. It didn't hit him.

Flash simply plucked it out of the air and sent it flying back. This time it hit her on the forehead.

"Ouch!" she said. "That left a mark!"

"It didn't, either. Besides, that's pine cone football."

Even in the middle of the game, Billy Rollins was complaining. "I want you to know I haven't forgotten that somebody took my compass."

"Why don't you give it a rest for a while, Billy!" Daniel Saville said. "I don't think you've done anything but complain since we've been out here."

Billy looked angry. Here was a newcomer telling him what to do.

"You mind your own business!" he said rudely, but then he said, "I know what I'm going to do. I'm going to search all of your knapsacks."

"You're not searching my knapsack!" Delores said.

"Mine, either!" Joe said. "Billy, give it a rest! Like Daniel says."

Just then Mr. Jones appeared. "Time to move out! We've got to make some tracks."

They started off again. Amos Redfield, a twelve-year-old homeschooler, started naming every plant and every tree that grew along the trail.

"That's angel hair there," he said. "And that's jack-in-the-pulpit."

"How do you know all this stuff?" Juliet asked. "You learn it out of books?"

"No. My dad taught me. He knows just about everything about plants."

"Do you know which plants are good to eat?" Joe asked.

"Sure!" Amos said. "Dandelions, for one thing."

"Dandelions! You mean the kind that you blow?"

"Yeah. You can make good soup out of the roots."

Juliet listened in amazement as Amos told about plants she had never heard of.

Mr. Tanner nodded his approval. "That's quite a knowledge of plants you've got there, Amos. Maybe you could teach the rest of the kids something."

"You seem to be the foliage expert," Mr. Gordon said with a grin. "If I tried to eat anything out here, I'd probably poison myself."

They crossed one shallow stream that presented some difficulty for Flash. Its rocky bed was hard on the wheelchair. But Joe took one wheel, Chili took the other, and Juliet pushed from behind, and they muscled him across.

Once Joe noticed a cave in the side of a hill. "That's a cave!" he cried. "Let's go inside!"

"We'd better not do that, Joe," their father warned.

"Why not?"

"Because there may be bats in there."

"Will a little old bat hurt you?"

"Some of them carry rabies. You have to be very careful around bats."

"Are they vampires?" Billy asked, his voice not quite steady.

"Oh no. Not in this part of the country, Billy. In parts of the world there are vampire bats that suck the blood out of cattle. But there's nothing like that around here," Mr. Jones assured him.

"Can't we just *look* in?" Joe begged.

"Better not."

"Why not?"

"This country doesn't have vampires, but it does have a few bears left in it. Sometimes they hole up in these caves."

Juliet shivered. "I wouldn't want to meet a bear."

"Aw, they won't hurt you if they're little black bears," Chili said. "I read that in a book."

"But it might not be a black bear. And it

might not be *little*. It might be a grizzly bear," Flash said.

"Not around here," Mr. Jones said. "Hasn't been a grizzly around here in many years."

Later they did find one good-sized cave that was more open. It was not very deep, and they stopped to play in it. The men decided to set up camp by the cave opening.

"Looks like rain," Juliet said.

"And we've got to find something to eat before it does," Mr. Tanner said. "Any of you know how to make snares for rabbits?"

Nobody did, but Mr. Tanner showed them.

To Juliet's—and everyone else's—surprise, they caught four rabbits that day. Amos Redfield gathered a bunch of greens, so they had rabbit stew and a green salad for supper. Some of the leaders had brought some granola bars for dessert. Although nobody really had enough, they were learning to live in the woods.

The rain never came, and the men built up a big fire. Then Mr. Jones said, "And now we're going to have a contest."

"What kind of a contest?" Juliet asked.

"A contest to see who can tell the scariest ghost story."

A cheer went up, but Jenny said, "I get nervous about ghost stories, especially at night."

"Oh, it's all right," Joe said. "I won't let them get you."

"What would you do if a bear came to get me?" Juliet asked him.

"I'd skin him," Joe said cheerfully. He pulled out his pocketknife. "No bear better come around me."

"I doubt if that'd do the job, Son," his father said. "But let's get on with the story-telling."

First, Flash told a story about a man with a hook for a hand, coming through the woods and grabbing someone at night.

He built up the suspense, finally saying slowly, "And then this girl . . . heard . . . something . . . coming . . ."

It was very quiet. Only the crackling of the fire could be heard. Juliet was sitting next to his wheelchair, and she shivered. She was remembering the night before when *she* had heard something in the woods.

"And then suddenly—" Flash grabbed Juliet by the shoulder.

"Yaaaaa!"

Everyone around the campfire burst into laughter, for Juliet had screamed at the top of her lungs.

"That wasn't very funny, Flash!"

"I thought it was," Joe said. "I didn't know you could move so fast or yell so loud."

Joe's story was about a large black bear that came into a camp for food.

"And this big black bear, he wanted some-

40

thing sweet." Joe looked around, grinning. "He didn't find any candy bars, so he had to eat up one of the girls, because they're so sweet."

After the laughter quieted down, Jenny said, "I'm glad you know that girls are sweet and boys are sour."

The storytelling contest went on until at last Mr. Jones said, "We'd better get to bed. No tents tonight. You girls sleep back in the cave."

"Yeah, we guys are going to sleep outside under the stars," Billy Rollins said.

Camping out was so different from sleeping in a house. Juliet thought. Everybody's gear was unpacked and lying all around. It was fun getting ready to sleep.

"Oh, it's been a wonderful day!" Juliet sighed and snuggled down in her sleeping bag. Jenny was on one side of her and Delores on the other.

"It sure has been," Delores said. "The air smells so nice in the woods."

"Listen to the boys talking out there. I wonder what they're talking about."

"Oh, boys don't ever talk about anything important."

Once in a while Juliet could hear what they were saying.

Joe said something about the wild animals that they might have to kill.

"Yeah," Billy said, "and those girls are going to be useless for that. They couldn't kill anything."

"I don't know if you could either, Billy." That was Jack Tanner's voice.

"You just wait and see! And you watch what I tell you—when we start rock climbing, they're going to be pitiful!"

Juliet sniffed at that. Then the voices began to grow softer. After a time the conversation stopped. She drifted off to sleep.

Juliet woke up, not knowing why.

She listened carefully and thought she heard a rustling sound.

I'll bet that's Billy and Jack and some of those boys, she thought. *I'll bet they're going to play a trick on us.* She was about to yell out for them to go to sleep but decided that would wake everybody up. Instead, she reached down into her sleeping bag for her penlight, got up, and went to the mouth of the cave. She flashed the light in the direction of the sound.

"Who's that?" she whispered. She caught a glimpse of something, or someone, leaving the camping area off to her right. Her heart began to thump. It was cloudy and very dark. The campfire was still glowing. Apparently, everyone was asleep except for her.

Juliet thought about going toward where she had seen something moving but then decided to go back to bed.

42

She zipped up the sleeping bag, then lay awake for a long time. Finally she thought, *I don't want anyone to think I'm letting my imagination run away with me. People always say that.*

As a matter of fact, Juliet did have a vivid imagination. More than once she'd gotten into difficulties because of it. *I don't know what that sound was. It may have been just an animal.* Still, she could not go to sleep. *That's twice I've heard something—or somebody,* she thought. *I can't imagine what it is.*

She finally drifted off, only to dream about black bears and ghosts with hooks for arms. Then she dreamed about eating granola. From time to time she almost woke up but never quite. Too Smart Jones was too tired to wake up again.

A Wounded Bird

The first thing Juliet heard the next morning was Billy Rollins. She came out of her sleeping bag, mumbling, "What's he fussing about now?"

"I don't know," Jenny said. "But let's go see."

By the time the girls had their boots on, Billy was shouting.

They joined the gathering crowd.

"What's the matter with him?" Jenny asked.

"He says somebody stole his canteen."

"That's right!" Billy said. His face was red, and he was waving his arms around. "First you stole my compass and now my canteen!"

"Who are you accusing?" Flash asked.

"I don't know! One of you did it, though! Don't you have anything better to do than to steal my stuff?" Billy carried on for quite a while.

Juliet found her group leader. "I thought I heard something last night, Mr. Harris. And the night before that, too."

"Why didn't you say something before?"

"Well . . . well . . ." Juliet was embarrassed. "You see, Mr. Harris, I've been accused of having too much imagination."

He grinned. "So have I. But still, if you really heard something, maybe you should have told me."

"Well, I decided it was just an animal I heard. But then last night I thought I *saw* something."

Mr. Harris listened while Juliet related her experiences. Then he said, "Juliet, just keep this to yourself for now."

"Oh, I will!"

"I'll check it out, but it's better not to get everybody upset."

"I know. Especially Billy Rollins."

"I've heard of raccoons taking things out of camp," he went on. "Shiny objects and things like that. I wonder if it could have been a coon."

"I don't know. I didn't see anything close."

"Well, just keep it to yourself," he repeated. "I'll keep an eye out."

Breakfast that morning was leftover rabbit stew and some berries that the girls had gathered the previous day, along with the ever present granola bars.

"I'm so sick of granola bars," Juliet said. "I hope I never see another one."

"By the time this week's over," Joe said, "you may be glad to get them."

"All right, everybody. We're ready to go!" Chili once again was running ahead of the others to "blaze the trail."

The group leaders pointed out interesting things along the way. Some of the youngsters picked up leaves, and stones, and strange looking pieces of wood for their collections.

When the trail took them alongside a high hill, Juliet said, "I'm glad we don't have to climb *that!*"

"No," Mr. Harris said, "but here's where you're going to learn to do a little mountain climbing." He pulled off his backpack and began to take out ropes. "We've got to be very careful. This is not a particularly steep hill, but someone still could get hurt. So we're going to go very slow."

"I'll go first," Chili said. "I always thought I'd make a great mountain climber."

Soon everyone was yelling as Chili began ascending the hill. He had a rope tied around his waist. Mr. Tanner was at the top, pulling. Mr. Harris was at the bottom, holding a trailing rope and giving advice.

Everyone had to have a try at it after that, even Flash.

"I don't see how Flash can go up in that wheelchair," Joe whispered.

But Flash did not attempt to climb. He had a very strong upper body, so he held the rope while Mr. Harris went up. "Hey, this is cool!" he said. "Come on, Billy. Let's see what kind of a mountain climber you are."

"I'm the best! That's what I am!" Billy said. But he seemed unsure when he looked up the hill. "You guys hold onto that rope, you hear me?"

"We will!" Flash said. "You'll be all right."

Billy tied the rope securely around his middle.

Up at the top, Mr. Tanner called, "Don't you worry, Billy. We won't let you fall."

"Be sure of that!"

"Oh, go on!" Flash said. "I've got this rope, and Mr. Tanner's got the other one."

Slowly Billy began to climb.

Flash suddenly looked at Juliet and said, "Let's give Billy a thrill." He began pulling the rope to one side and then to the other.

"Hey, what are you doing?" Billy yelled.

"Nothing!" Flash said. However, he soon had Billy screaming at the top of his lungs.

"Enjoy yourself, Billy!" Flash called. "You're a great rock climber!"

Finally Billy got to the top, and then Jack went up. Flash pulled the rope sideways for him too, but Jack seemed to like it, for he asked for more.

Later, though, Juliet heard Mr. Harris have a quiet word with Flash about never, never, never deliberately scaring people when they're rock climbing.

After about two hours, the rock climbing lesson was over. Leaders and all sat down for a break and snacked on the inevitable granola bars. They talked about what they had learned and soon were on their way through the woods again.

"I still don't understand about Billy's compass and canteen," Juliet said.

Samuel was tramping alongside Juliet. "I don't, either. I do know Billy does things just to get attention sometimes."

"But he wouldn't do a thing like that, would he?" Kelsey Saville asked.

"Billy likes attention. He'll get it any way he can."

"Are you having a good time on this outing, Kelsey?" Delores asked her.

"Oh yes! I just wish we'd see more animals. Especially birds. I love birds."

"I hope we don't see any bears," Juliet said.

"I wouldn't want to see any of those either," Kelsey said quickly, "but I'd like to see a deer."

"I saw some tracks yesterday," Joe said. "They were fresh too."

The campers hiked on. Juliet was thinking

again about the noises that she had heard, when behind her Kelsey cried, "Listen!"

"What's the matter?" Daniel asked.

"I heard something in the woods!"

"Something scary? What did it sound like?"

"No—more like a chirping sound."

"Probably a bird, then. Or a squirrel. Come on, Kelsey. We have to keep up."

"It was a bird, I know. That's what it was."

Juliet stopped to wait for them. She could tell that Kelsey was very interested in what she had heard.

"Maybe it *was* a bird," Juliet said. "We could take time to just look."

They stepped off the trail under the trees, and right away Kelsey exclaimed, "Here it is!"

Juliet saw her pick up something. "What is it?"

"It's a bird, and there's something wrong with it."

Daniel leaned close. "It's young. Hasn't learned how to fly yet. Looks like its wing is hurt."

"We've got to take it with us," Kelsey said. "And make it better."

"We can't do that!" Daniel exclaimed. "Not on an overnight camping trip!"

"I can. I can take care of it."

Juliet squinted at the brown bird. "What kind is it?"

"I don't know, but see how pretty he is?"

Kelsey pulled off her hat and put the injured bird very carefully into it. She cuddled it close as they went back to join the others.

Sooner or later everyone had to have a look at the baby bird.

Billy said, "That bird would make a nice lunch for somebody."

"You hush, Billy Rollins!" Kelsey cried.

He laughed. "Don't worry. He wouldn't be enough lunch for anybody."

Mr. Tanner even brought out the first aid kit. They all watched as he put a bandage on the little bird's hurt wing.

"We'll take turns carrying him," Juliet offered.

The day got surprisingly warm later, and when the group came to a narrow stream, Juliet said, "Let's go wading!"

That suited everyone—except Billy.

"I'm not putting my stuff down! There's a thief among us."

"Well, you stay here and sit on your stuff, Billy," Joe said. "The rest of us will have fun."

The leaders sat down on the ground and watched as the boys and girls waded, splashed, and kicked the water.

Flash Gordon had had a tiring day. It was hard rolling the wheelchair even where the trail was good. But even he got into the water and was able to splash some on the others.

When they made camp later in the day, Kelsey found some worms and fed the little bird. Juliet sat beside her, watching.

"I hope his wing will get all right," Kelsey said.

"Oh, I think it will. We can take him to the people at the Nature Preserve when we get back. They'll know what to do."

"Birds don't have much chance when they're this small. They can't take care of themselves," Kelsey said. "I always feel sorry for them."

"So do I, but this one's going to be all right. I can tell."

"I always liked that part in the Bible where it says God knows when a sparrow falls."

"I like that part too. If He cares about sparrows—think how much He must love us."

The two girls sat talking as Kelsey held the bird. Then they went to the campfire and sang songs with the others.

Billy kept his backpack close by his side. "I'm going to use this for a pillow!" he declared. "Nobody is going to steal anything else of mine!"

"I sure don't know who wants your old stuff!" Joe grumbled.

By bedtime, Juliet was so tired she thought she would go to sleep at once. But she got to thinking about the bird. She hoped it would be all right. Then she thought about Billy. *I feel sorry for Billy,* she thought. *He's his own worst enemy. He'd be a nice guy if he just tried.*

She heard a distant barking. Somebody's dog. Next she heard an owl hooting. She *thought* it was an owl. He was close. Juliet lifted her head, hoping to catch a glimpse of him.

I can't see anything from back in here. She got out of the sleeping bag and tiptoed to the mouth of the cave.

Suddenly there was a frantic scrambling in the underbrush. *This time I know I heard something!* She moved toward the sound but could see nothing.

If there only was a full moon, she thought. *It's too dark to see anything!*

Juliet went back to her sleeping bag. She took out her penlight, found her journal, and began to write.

I'm going to write it all down—everything strange that's happened. They'll make fun of me if I say anything about a mystery. But something funny is going on.

When Juliet had written down everything she could think of, with a sigh of relief she turned off the penlight and lay back and closed her eyes.

"I'm going to start my detective work first thing in the morning," she whispered.

The Mystery Deepens

The first thing Jenny did when she got out of her sleeping bag was to wash her face in the stream. The morning air was nippy and the water was very cold, so bathing was out of the question. But she'd been waiting for Billy to tease her about roughing it, so she determined not to complain.

When she got back to the cave, Delores was already gone, and Juliet was up and packing.

"Go on down to the brook, Juliet." Jenny smiled innocently. "Nothing like hot water on a crisp November day."

"I'll bet!" Juliet ran a hand through her hair and made a face. "I'll never get these tangles out."

Jenny touched her own hair and nodded. "That would be one good thing about being a boy. They don't have to worry about their hair."

"I don't care. Who wants to be an old boy anyway?"

"Not me. Here, let me brush out some of those tangles."

Juliet sat quietly while Jenny brushed her hair. She was thinking, as usual, about the mystery that had developed. When Jenny said, "OK. That's about as good as we can do it," Juliet said, "Let me do yours now."

She began to brush Jenny's tangles. "You have pretty hair."

"It's red! And I'm so tired of getting teased. How many times have I heard Billy say, 'Redheaded peckerwood sittin' on a fence, tryin' to make a dollar out of fifteen cents'?"

"That's mean."

"And he thinks that kind of teasing is so clever."

"Now you know how I feel when they call me 'Too Smart Jones.'"

"That's mean, too. And Billy never misses a chance."

"Never."

"What do you suppose happened to his compass and canteen?"

"I can't figure it out—unless he was just careless and lost them somewhere. But that's not like Billy, either."

By now Jenny was rummaging around in

her knapsack. She sat back with a puzzled look. "Juliet?"

"What?"

"I hate to tell you this."

"Hate to tell me what?"

"Well—" Jenny's face had an odd expression "—my favorite barrette is missing."

"Not that pretty one your mother gave you for your birthday?"

"Yes. It was valuable, too. It had mother-of-pearl insets."

"It's got to be there. You were wearing it yesterday."

"I know I was. But I can't find it. Help me look."

The two girls went through every pocket of Jenny's backpack. Then they searched the cave.

"Could it have fallen out while you were in the woods?"

"No, I took it off last night and put it right by my other things."

The girls looked at each other. Juliet didn't know what to think.

When they went over to the campfire, Billy said, "What's the matter? You two look like you swallowed a frog."

"It's—my barrette," Jenny answered.

"What about your old barrette?"

"It's gone."

Billy snorted. "You see! Now you know how I feel getting stuff stolen!"

The other boys and girls stood around listening, and Joe said, "We'll all help you look for it. Maybe it's in the cave."

"It's not there." Juliet said firmly. "We looked all over the place. It's just gone."

"Well, this is a pretty come-off!" Flash muttered. "What do you make out of it?"

"Don't ask me." Chili pointed toward Juliet. "There's the detective right there. Start detecting, Too Smart!"

"Don't call me that, Chili!"

"Oh, sorry about that. I forgot."

But Juliet's mind was not really on what Chili was saying. She was thinking of something else. She said thoughtfully, "The things that have been taken are things that aren't very heavy . . ." She thought a little more. "And all of them had sort of a shine to them . . ."

"That's right. So?"

"They were things that could have glittered in the firelight . . ." Juliet went on.

At that moment Mr. Tanner came up. "What's going on so early?" he asked.

"Somebody's taken Jenny's barrette."

"Really? Well, if that's true, it's pretty serious."

By that time the rest of the leaders had joined them, and there was a great deal of talk about things being taken. Mr. Rollins made a long speech about honesty. He finished by saying, "Of all the places where we shouldn't have to worry about things like this, it's out here in the woods!"

"I wish he wouldn't go on like that," Juliet said. "It doesn't do any good."

"I guess he's just worried," Delores answered. "Who knows what will disappear next?"

Juliet never really forgot about Jenny's missing barrette that day, but several interesting things happened so that she put it in the back of her mind.

For one thing, the hikers stopped to check out fossil leaves in some big rocks.

"I know what we can do!" Joe said excitedly.

"What? Take the rocks home with us?" Billy asked.

"That's crazy!" Flash said. "They're too big!"

"We can't take the rocks, but we can make rubbings of them," Joe said. "I'll show you."

All the boys and girls had brought tablets to keep journals. It was part of their wilderness experience. Joe tore off a sheet from his and then took out a pencil. With his pocketknife, he began shaving the lead onto the paper. When he had a tiny pile, he held the paper against a rock. He began to press it down so that the imprints of the ancient leaves showed on the surface.

"See?" he said when he was through. "I'll

bet you this will win a prize at the science fair."

"Aw, that's no good!" Billy said. He pulled out his ax and advanced toward the rocks. "Let's bust up one and take it home!"

"No, we can't do that," Mr. Tanner said quickly. "Too many old things like this are being spoiled."

"We wouldn't spoil anything," Billy protested. "We'd just take it back, and people could look at it."

Mr. Tanner put his arm around Billy's shoulder. "Let's leave it here for the next visitors that come along. They can see it in the natural."

Billy grumbled, but he stuck his ax back into its sheath on his belt.

Then everybody wanted to try making a rubbing of the fossils.

Juliet was watching Flash and Chili work when Flash said, "I wish I could find a dinosaur skeleton."

Chili looked up. "Wouldn't it be something to find a T-rex?"

"Wonder what it was like to live when those things were around. They could eat you up in one gulp."

"Yeah. Did you see that movie about 'em?"

"Sure. About three times."

The two were so busy talking about lizards and dinosaurs that they both jumped when Juliet's father tapped each boy on the shoulder.

"Don't scare me like that, Mr. Jones!" Chili yelped.

"Well, I like to see boys interested in what they're doing, but we've got to get along. And Chili, you're the trailbreaker."

"Yes, sir!"

The group moved on with Chili at the front. Juliet and several others had brought cameras—the throwaway kind. She'd stop to take pictures from time to time. Once when she'd stopped, she cried, "There's some animal in those bushes!"

Several of the boys advanced slowly. Billy took out his ax, saying, "Just let me at it! I'll kill it, whatever it is!"

"Maybe it's a rattlesnake," Joe said slyly.

Billy stopped abruptly. "Snake!" Then he said, "No, can't be a snake. It's too cold for snakes."

"Not too cold for the icy diamondback. They live in ice all the time."

Juliet knew Chili was teasing.

But Billy was not taking any chances. He backed away.

Then Chili said, "Come on, Flash. Let's flush this thing out."

The two boys crept toward the bushes, and suddenly something scurried out.

"It's an armadillo!" Chili yelled.

Juliet managed to snap a picture of the

scaly little animal as it hurried away. "That ought to come out nice," she said.

"Do you know what's odd about armadillos?" Amos asked.

"What's odd about armadillos?"

"Whenever a mother armadillo has a litter, they're either all males or all females."

"How do you know stuff like that?" she asked.

"I read it someplace," Amos answered in his shy way. "And you know how you see armadillos beside the road—killed by cars?"

"Sure. Happens all the time."

"A lot of the time it's their own fault," Amos said. "It's their defense mechanism."

"What's that?" Flash asked curiously.

"When they're startled, armadillos jump straight up in the air. I mean just straight up. If they'd just scoot down when a car comes, the wheels might go on either side of them. But they jump up, so the bumper catches them."

"They ought to take a class in armadillo safety," Billy said. "Come on, Jack. Let's see if we can catch that critter."

"We've got better things to do right now," Mr. Tanner said. "We're going to try to catch some squirrels for supper."

"Some squirrel stew sounds all right!" Chili said. "Maybe we can even make some chili. I've never had squirrel chili."

"Ugh!" Juliet said. "Squirrels are so cute the way they sit up on their hind legs. I don't think I could eat one."

"You don't have any trouble eating hamburgers. They come from cute little calves," her brother said.

"Yeah, and you don't mind eating lamb. They're cute too," Samuel put in.

Juliet knew she was not being quite logical. "I don't care! I just couldn't eat a frisky little squirrel."

That afternoon the boys did trap several rabbits and squirrels—with the help of the leaders.

"I don't know how you clean a squirrel," Joe said.

"I do!" And Daniel proceeded to do it with some adult supervision.

It took quite a while to get all this done. By the time they had eaten, Juliet glanced at the clouds and said, "It looks like rain."

"We'd better set up those tents. I don't want to sleep in a mud puddle," Joe agreed.

The tents were quickly put up, for they had all learned how to cooperate on that job.

At bedtime the crickets down by the creek began to sing.

"I love to hear crickets," Delores said. She was sleeping between Juliet and Jenny tonight. "They sound like they practice singing together."

"I love the sounds when we're outdoors like

this," Juliet said. "And the stars twinkling . . ." She looked out the tent flap. "Look up there. Millions and millions of stars."

"The Bible says God knows every one of them by name, too," Jenny said. "That's a lot of names to remember."

"It wouldn't be hard for God. He made them all. Why wouldn't He know their names?"

The girls lay talking for quite a while, and finally Juliet dozed off.

She did not know how long she had been asleep, but she came awake with a start, for a hand was gripping her shoulder!

She saw it was Jenny. "What is it?"

"*Ssh.*" Jenny was sitting up and peering out into the darkness in front of the tent. "There's something out there."

Now Delores was awake. All three girls sat staring into the dark. There was some star-light, and it had not rained yet, but Juliet could really see nothing.

"What did it sound like, Jenny?" she asked.

"I don't know exactly, but I think we'd better investigate. You think we should get some of the men?"

Delores said no. "We're just going outside the tent. If anything happens, we can always scream."

The three girls pulled on their boots and tiptoed out into the night.

"I don't see anything," Juliet said.

"I don't, either," Jenny whispered. "Wait! Look over there!"

Juliet caught just a glimpse of movement. "What is it? I can't see very well."

"I don't know," Delores said. "But I don't think we'd better go after it, whatever it is. It might be a wolf."

"We'd better for sure go tell my dad," Juliet said.

Juliet's father sat up at once when she touched his shoulder. "What's wrong?"

"We saw something out there," Juliet said.

"What did you see?" Mr. Harris sat up, too. Soon all of the leaders were awake.

Juliet kept saying, "I don't know what it was. We couldn't see very well."

The talking soon awoke the boys, and then everybody was up. Flashlights popped on.

Juliet said, "Well, whoever or whatever it was would be gone now with all this racket."

Jack Tanner suddenly cried, "Oh no!"

"What is it, Son?" his father asked.

"My knife!"

As everybody gathered around, Juliet had to lean forward to see. Jack's leather sheath lay on top of his backpack, but the knife itself was gone.

"Somebody took my knife, Dad!" Jack wailed. "I can't believe it. It was right beside my head."

The usual questions started then. "When

did you have it last? Are you sure you didn't lose it in the woods?"

Jack was walking around in a circle looking at the ground. He was almost in tears. "Dad, that's the knife you gave me for Christmas last year. It's the best knife that ever was."

"Now don't get excited, Son. I'm sure there's an answer to all this."

"There's only one answer," Billy said. "There's a thief in this camp! Just like I've been telling you."

There was silence then, and Juliet felt a sick sensation in her stomach. She hated to think that one of their own homeschoolers would be a thief. But it certainly looked that way.

"We can't do anything tonight," Mr. Jones said. "Everybody go back to bed. We'll talk about this tomorrow. I'm sure there's a logical explanation."

It took some time to get everyone back in place, though.

"I don't think I can sleep a wink," Juliet said.

"Me either." Delores shivered. "Just think. Something might come right into this tent."

Jenny said, "It's really sad. This seems worse than the stolen bicycles."

"It *is* worse," Juliet said. "Those were professional thieves, but we know everyone here.

I can't believe any of us would take things like this."

Jenny said, very thoughtfully, "And whoever it is knows everything about the rest of us. They knew I loved that barrette. And they knew Jack loved that knife."

"And they knew Billy loved that compass," Juliet said. "I'm starting to wish we hadn't come on this trip. I'm afraid we're going to find out something bad about one of us."

Juliet Is Accused

Sunday morning dawned with bright sunshine. As usual, the campers rose and washed their faces in the cold water of the stream.

As Juliet brushed her hair, she said, "Weekdays are so different out here in the woods, but Sundays are still the same."

Jenny finished her own hair, then turned to Juliet. "Here, let me help you with that," she said. "I feel that way, too. It's still worship day, but it'll be funny going to church outside and not in a building."

When the girls went outside, Juliet smelled the delicious aroma of frying meat.

"Hi. Come on over," Flash called. He was sitting next to the campfire watching Chili and Samuel cook something in a big frying pan.

"Fresh squirrel and rabbit for breakfast.

How about that?" Samuel said. "Us men are the best cooks, I always say."

"Oh sure!" Flash agreed. "The big hotels, they all have men chefs. I never heard of a chefette."

Juliet knew that they were teasing, but she did not care. She was ready for whatever they were cooking. "As long as I get something good to eat, you can say anything you want."

Before long, everyone was enjoying a better-than-usual breakfast. Juliet's father had found a large number of quail eggs, and the campers said they tasted great.

"These are better than chicken eggs!" Billy said. "Give me some more!"

"Mr. Jones didn't find enough eggs to supply the whole world!" Jack Tanner told him.

Immediately after breakfast, Mr. Jones said, "And now it's time for church. Suppose we begin with a song service. Jenny, we're going to let you choose the hymns today."

Juliet knew her dad said that because Jenny had a beautiful voice.

Right away, Jenny said, "I want to sing, 'What a Friend We Have in Jesus.'"

"That's a good one," said Mr. Jones. "Start it, Jenny, and the rest of us will just jump in."

Jenny—and then the rest—began singing:

"What a Friend we have in Jesus,
All our sins and griefs to bear.

70

What a privilege to carry
Everything to God in prayer.
O what peace we often forfeit,
O what needless pain we bear,
All because we do not carry
Everything to God in prayer."

"How about 'The Old Rugged Cross'?" Jack Tanner suggested. "That's my favorite."

Jenny at once began singing. She had a clear voice, and she loved to sing.

"On a hill far away stood an old rugged cross,
  The emblem of suffering and shame.
  And I love that old cross where the dearest and best
  For a world of lost sinners was slain."

The woods rang with the sound of their singing. It was chilly, but the sun was beginning to warm the earth. As the homeschoolers and their leaders gathered in a circle, Juliet whispered to Delores, "Church is good anywhere, isn't it?"

"Yes. I've never been at a church like this."

"Neither have I. It just shows that it's not the building that makes a church. It's the people."

That thought turned out to be the subject of Mr. Jones's talk. He had been chosen to bring the "sermon," although he was not a preacher.

"In Psalm 90," he began, "Moses said, 'Lord, thou hast been our dwelling place in all generations.' And that's what I want to talk to you about.

"The people of Israel were wandering from place to place with their flocks. At night they would sleep in tents. They didn't have houses. But Moses said an important thing here. It was as if he said, 'We don't have houses made of stone or wood, but we do have a house. It is the Lord God. We live in Him. He is our dwelling place.'"

Juliet's dad looked around the circle. "Many of God's people have had to say that. Millions of Christians have been driven from their homes by persecution. But they can remember what Moses said. God is their dwelling place."

Mr. Jones ended his talk by saying, "I hope we all remember that if we lose everything we have, if we lose the houses we live in, all the clothes, all the things we enjoy most, we still have the Lord."

When their outdoor church was over, Mr. Tanner said, "And now it's time to move out. We've got a lot to do today."

Everybody began milling around. They were up to the fifth day of their adventure, and most still seemed excited about it.

"Where are we going today?" Juliet asked her father.

"We're going to show you something that some of you have never seen before."

"What's that?" Billy asked loudly.

"Wait and see. It won't take long."

The trail wound past big trees and thick undergrowth. Flash needed a lot of help with his wheelchair. They all worked together, however, and before long Jack Tanner was saying, "I hear something!"

Juliet stopped walking and turned her head to one side. "I hear something, too. It sounds like water running."

"Keep going. You'll see what it is." Her father led them around a bend in the trail, and suddenly they were standing at the bottom of a steep bluff. Over the top of it was falling a cascade of water. The sound they had heard was the water falling into the pool at the bottom.

"A waterfall!" Samuel Del Rio exclaimed.

"I've never seen one before," Flash said.

"Can we get under it and let it fall over us?" Delores cried.

Mr. Jones laughed. "Not in this kind of weather, Delores. Maybe next summer, when it's warm, we can come back. That would make a good swimming hole, all right."

Everyone was fascinated by the waterfall. They stood watching it for a long time.

Joe said, "This water makes me think of something. It's going to be great making that canoe trip down through the rapids! There's whitewater down there."

"Water's not white!" Billy said.

"That shows what you know." Joe grinned. He always loved to show up Billy Rollins. "Whitewater's when the water's so fast and rough that you see the little white caps."

"Oh, I knew that," Billy said.

"You didn't either. You just asked what's whitewater."

Billy could never stand to be corrected. He punched Joe on the arm.

"Ow! Don't you do that again!" Joe yelled.

"You two stop picking on each other," Juliet ordered. "Let's just have fun and not fight."

Billy turned to her and laughed. "Well, look who's talking! Too Smart Jones!"

"Billy, if you call me that one more time, I'll—I'll—"

"What will you do? Shove me in the river?"

"No, I won't shove you in the river, but I wish you'd stop calling me that."

Everyone was listening now, and Billy was the center of attention. "You know what I think? I think Too Smart Jones can't find any mysteries to solve out here so she made up one."

"What are you talking about?" Samuel asked.

"I mean she just created this mystery about missing things."

"How could she do that?" Joe said. "You're crazy, Billy Rollins!"

"No, I'm not! I'll tell you what she's done." Billy looked around at his audience. "*She's* taken all of our stuff—especially mine, because she's jealous of what I have."

"I am not!" Juliet said furiously.

"Sure you are! You're jealous because I have better things than you do. You're just jealous."

"That's the craziest thing I ever heard of! I never wanted anything you had!"

"And what's more," Billy said, "I'll bet if we searched her backpack, we'd find all our missing things in there."

The grownups stood a little distance away, still looking at the waterfall. Billy called, "Hey, Mr. Harris!"

Mr. Harris came back. "What is it, Billy?"

"I think we ought to search Juliet's backpack."

"What are you talking about?"

"I'm talking about I think she took all our things and stuffed them in her backpack."

Mr. Harris just looked at Billy. "That's a serious thing to say about anybody. Why would Juliet do that?"

"I know her better than you do. She always has to be the center of attention."

"*You're* the one that has to be the center of

75

attention," Joe said. His face was red, and he said, "Mr. Harris, he's crazy!"

"No, I'm not! Just open that backpack of hers. You'll find the stuff in there."

Mr. Harris turned to Juliet with a sigh. "Well, Juliet. What do you say? You heard what Billy said."

"I don't care. I know there's nothing in there that's missing. Go ahead and look." Juliet took off her backpack and handed it to Mr. Harris.

He began to take out the items. He named them off as he removed them.

Juliet said, "I know *somebody's* taking this stuff, but it's not me."

Mr. Harris finally had everything out for display. Then he turned to Billy. "You see anything that's been missing, Billy?"

"Aw, she hid them somewhere," Billy said weakly.

"I think you owe Juliet an apology, Billy." Mr. Harris sounded stern.

"Yeah . . . well . . . I was wrong—about this, anyway," Billy mumbled.

"That's not much of an apology," Joe said.

Billy stuck out his tongue at Juliet and then turned quickly and walked away.

Joe said. "Why does he always have to act like that?"

"I don't know," Juliet said. "Sometimes I think he's the most unhappy boy I know."

"He's never satisfied unless everybody's looking at him."

"Anyway, that takes you off the hook, Juliet," Flash said cheerfully. "Now we can get on with the program."

"Yeah, it's going to be a big hike today," Chili said. He came over to Juliet. "Don't worry about what Billy Rollins says."

Juliet said, "Thank you, Chili. It's always good to get an encouraging word."

"OK, everybody," Chili said. "Let's get on with it. We've got a trail to get through."

Visitor
in the Camp

Let me give you a hand, Flash."

Mr. Jones grabbed the handles of Flash Gordon's wheelchair and tilted it back.

The hikers were winding along a twisting trail by the side of a steep hill. Flash ordinarily did not like to be helped, but this time he leaned back, saying, "It's nice to have a chauffeur."

Juliet laughed. "You've got it good, just sitting there while the rest of us have to walk."

"Yep. I always demand the best for myself."

Juliet and Joe both helped ease the wheelchair down a steep place.

"I can handle it from here!" Flash said. "It's clear sailing!"

"Well, OK. But don't go too fast."

"There's no such thing as too fast," Flash yelped. "Let's go!" He spun the wheels, and they watched him fly down the trail.

Juliet thought of what Flash often said. "He says the Lord's going to get him out of that wheelchair one of these days."

By now, most were showing their fatigue in one way or another. Juliet and the other girls lagged behind a bit, and even the boys were quieter than usual.

When they came to a small stream winding alongside the trail, Juliet said, "Let's get a drink of water." In seconds, the whole group was spread out beside the brook. Some dipped up water with their canteen cups, but Samuel simply lay flat on his stomach and drank thirstily.

"This is better than any water in town," he announced.

Then Amos said, "I see some bloodroot!"

"What's bloodroot?" Joe asked.

Amos gave him an unbelieving look. "You don't know what bloodroot is?"

"I don't have any idea. What is it?"

"This is it!" Amos pulled up a white wild-flower that had rounded leaves. He said, "A long time ago, the Indians liked this."

"What did they do with it? Eat it?"

"No, no. When you break the stem, it oozes out this juice. It looks like blood." As the others surrounded him, Amos put a few drops on his finger. "They used it to decorate their faces for battle. Like this." He drew a red line across his forehead.

"Hey, I can do that! Let's put on our war paint!" Joe cried.

The boys began breaking the bloodroot stems and decorating their faces.

The girls would have none of that. "I don't want *my* face messed up!" Delores sniffed.

But the boys had a good time.

Juliet said, "It's fun to have somebody along who knows things like this, Amos."

"Show us some more," Joe urged.

"Well, this is pokeweed. Back in early America, everybody liked pokeweed because it was supposed to cure rheumatism."

"Is it good to eat?" Flash had smeared red lines across his forehead and down his cheeks, and he did look rather ferocious.

"Well, the big roots are poisonous," Amos told them. "But when you get them young, you can boil them and eat 'em like asparagus."

"Wow, I wouldn't want to eat anything that could be poisonous," Juliet said. "I think I'd just rather have asparagus."

Amos grinned. "The early settlers couldn't run down to the grocery store and buy asparagus. They had to eat roots and things like that. Besides, they taste pretty good."

"You mean you've eaten them?"

"Sure. My dad and I go out and get some every spring."

When everyone was rested, they moved along. Soon Mr. Tanner was saying, "I think we'd better try to get something to eat. How about some fish this time?"

"We don't have any bait," Jack said.

"I'll show you how to get some." His father took a net out of his backpack. "Here, Chili, you take the other end of this."

"OK. What are we doing?"

"Catching minnows."

Everybody else watched Mr. Tanner and Chili spread out the net and drag it along the bottom of the stream. When they drew up the net, it was full of minnows.

"We'll put them in this plastic jug—" Mr. Tanner had a small milk container in his backpack. It was punched with small holes in the top. He and Chili put the minnows inside. Then he said, "And now we'll catch some fish."

Juliet was always willing to fish. All the homeschoolers cut saplings for poles and spent the next hour fishing. The little stream was full of plump sun perch, and they caught enough for their noon meal. The fathers built a fire, and the girls helped fry the fish.

And then Chili was saying, "This way! Follow me!" It was time to move on.

The trail soon was running close to the edge of a cliff. Juliet looked down. It was a little cliff, but she thought it was a long way to the bottom.

Mr. Harris called, "Anyone want to try a little rappelling here?"

"Yeah!" the boys all shouted.

Juliet wasn't interested. She knew rappelling meant quickly going down a steep slope while holding onto a rope.

Mr. Harris took some equipment out of his pack. He tied up the rope used for rappelling, and he said, "OK, who's first?"

"Me!" Joe yelled. He stood at the top of the little cliff, and Mr. Harris showed him how to wrap the rope around his body. "Wrap it around your leg like this. It'll take all the strain, and you can let it out a little bit at a time."

Joe looked a little nervous, but he went down the incline in first-class order. When he was halfway, he even started yelling, "This is fun!"

One by one all the boys tried rappelling, and then the girls had to have their turn—even Juliet.

"Why don't we try some bungee jumping too?" Joe shouted.

But Mr. Jones shook his head. "I think that would be a little much."

Billy, of course, said that he was the best at rappelling, but Joe and Samuel laughed. Joe said, "Why did we have to pull you up then? You were too weak to do it by yourself."

"I was not!"

"Sure you were!"

That started a push-and-shove argument,

and the leaders had to break it up and calm everybody down.

Finally all were tired out from their hike and fishing expedition and rappelling, so they made camp for the night. Supper was roasted fish, baked wild potatoes, and berries, along with some pokeberry roots that Amos found.

Afterward they sat around the campfire and took turns telling stories again. Mr. Tanner told a story called "The Man with the Golden Arm." Some had heard it before, but those who hadn't were scared out of their wits when—at the exciting end of the story—Mr. Tanner suddenly yelled and threw himself at Billy Rollins.

Billy let out a wild scream and tried to get away.

Everyone else thought that was funny, but Billy began to sulk.

Joe said, "Don't feel bad, Billy. Everybody gets scared the first time they hear that story. I thought I'd jump out of my skin."

"That's a bad trick to play on a guy, Mr. Tanner," Billy complained.

"All in good fun, Billy. It's *meant* to be a scary story. Now, who wants to tell another one?"

They were sitting close to the fire, most of them wrapped in their sleeping bags for the air was chilly. The girls were the closest ring, the boys sat behind them, and then the adults.

"I bet that from the air we look just like a target," Chili joked. "A little circle, then a bigger circle, then the biggest circle."

"I like it out here in the woods," Juliet said. "We've got to do this again. It's been more fun than anything I've ever done in my life."

But Jenny looked tired. Her eyes were half closed. She said, "I don't think I'll even turn over tonight."

Indeed, before long, one by one, they all began to climb into their sleeping bags. The men stayed up longer than anyone else, and the sound of their voices lulled Too Smart Jones off into sleep.

Juliet woke up to the sound of the campfire's popping. She opened her eyes into mere slits. Every once in a while the logs shifted, and sparks would fly upward.

For a long time, she did not go back to sleep but was not fully awake either. She was thinking how much fun the outing had been, when her eyes caught a quick movement over to her right.

Juliet raised her head and looked. Then she started to get out of her sleeping bag. At the same moment, tin dishes went crashing somewhere.

"Hey, what's going on?" The voice was Joe's, and he came out of his sleeping bag, his hair messed up and his eyes foggy with sleep.

Samuel was fighting to get out of his bag, but he couldn't. The zipper must have been stuck. "Somebody help me get this thing open!"

Everything seemed to be happening at the same time, and the whole camp was soon standing around looking confused.

"What's going on here? What made that racket?" Mr. Jones looked at Juliet. "Is this some of your doing, Juliet?"

"No, but I did think I saw something just before all that noise."

All at once Mr. Tanner began to laugh. "There's your answer."

Everyone looked where he was pointing. It was a raccoon.

"Oh, isn't he darling!" Juliet said. "Look at that little mask he's got." She started toward the raccoon, but her father grabbed her arm.

"He might bite. He's wild, you know. Not like Boots."

They stood watching the raccoon. He did seem to be quite tame.

"Just remember that he's *not* tame," Mr. Jones said. "But now that he's found out where food is, he'll probably be back. We'll have to put all the edibles away, or he'll eat us out of house and home."

The men built up the fire again so that it sent bright sparks skyward. Everyone finally went back to bed.

Juliet squinted at her watch. "One thirty. It's the middle of the night!" Then she muttered to herself, "I wonder if it could have been a raccoon who took all those things. Maybe it was. They do that."

Far off a dog barked. Or perhaps it was a wolf. She shivered and pulled her head into the sleeping bag until only her nose stuck out. *I'll stay awake,* she thought. *If anything else is taken, I'll find out who's doing it.*

But she did not find out. As soon as this thought passed through her mind, Juliet was so tired that she drifted right off into sleep.

The Missing Cups

Morning came again and with it a light drizzle. It was not a soaking rain—just enough to make things uncomfortable.

Juliet crawled out of her sleeping bag. "Look, Jenny, my sleeping bag's all soggy."

"Mine too. But I guess that's the way it is when you sleep out in the rain."

The two girls went to wash their faces in the creek. Juliet suddenly laughed. "This is the longest I've ever gone without a bath."

"Me too." Jenny giggled.

"Joe's always said if nobody took baths, nobody would need to. But I never agreed with that. What I wouldn't give to get in a hot shower and wash my hair with some good shampoo."

"I guess that's not part of a 'wilderness experience,'" Jenny said. "We'll just have to wait until we get home."

After breakfast, Juliet walked over to where the leaders were doing some cleanup work. "Dad," she said, "I can wash the dishes in the creek."

"That's fine, Juliet. The quicker we get cleaned up, the quicker we can move on."

Juliet always liked to be helpful. She also wanted to prove to her father—and to Billy Rollins—that she was a good camper. She began gathering up the tin plates and cups.

"Wait a minute," she muttered. "This isn't everything. There are two more cups." They had brought exactly the right number, for they had not wanted to carry any more weight than necessary. "Someone has lost them, or maybe some of the men were drinking coffee out of them." Juliet began to look around. But she could not find the two cups.

"Joe, help me find a couple of cups."

"What cups?"

"There are two cups missing."

"Dad and Mr. Tanner probably had them, drinking coffee."

"Maybe so. I'll go ask them."

Juliet found her father. "Dad, did you have a cup over here? There are two of them missing."

"No. They're probably around somewhere, though."

"I've looked once, but I'll look again." She began making a circle of the camp, thinking that maybe someone had just set the cups down somewhere.

Suddenly Juliet stopped. She looked down at her feet and gasped. Then she began to yell, "Dad! Dad! Come here!"

Her calling must have been louder than she thought, because not only her dad but nearly everyone else hurried toward her.

"What are you yelling about now?" Billy asked.

Ignoring him, Juliet said, "Look at that!"

As everyone gathered around, Mr. Jones said, "That looks like a bear print. But it couldn't be . . ."

"Bears!" Delores cried. "You mean there are *bears* here? I'll never sleep again if I know there's a bear roaming around!"

Jenny looked nervous also. She held onto Mr. Tanner's arm. "Dad, let's leave here. We don't want to be where bears are."

Juliet was not too keen on bears herself, but she knew this was no time to get hysterical. "Maybe it's not a bear print after all. It's not very clear."

"This certainly isn't the right country for bears," Mr. Jones said thoughtfully.

Joe was still looking down at the bear track. He did not look too confident himself.

Sure enough, Billy had a remark to make. "Aw, a bear doesn't make that kind of print!"

Chili looked at it and frowned. "That's a

mighty big track. I'd hate to meet a bear that size."

"You know what I think?" Juliet said. "I think somebody just made that print to fool us."

"Like who?" Billy asked.

"Like you!"

"Me! Why are you picking on me?"

"You're mad because you had your compass and your canteen stolen!"

"You're crazy! You're not so smart after all, Too Smart Jones!"

"You might as well confess, Billy. You did it, didn't you?"

"Yeah," Joe said. "You've been acting awful ever since this business started. I bet it was you!"

Billy jumped on Joe. In seconds the two were rolling on the ground. Joe yelled and scuffled, trying to throw him off.

Mr. Jones and Mr. Rollins separated the boys.

"I'm ashamed of you!" Mr. Rollins said, holding onto Billy.

"It's her fault! Too Smart Jones said I made that bear track!"

"Well, he *could* have!" Juliet said. Actually, she was sorry she had said that and was ready to apologize.

But Billy was yelling. "She's the one that's always getting mysteries stirred up! It was probably her that made that track!"

"Wait a minute now!" Mr. Jones said. "Let's stop throwing accusations around. After all, nobody has any proof of anything."

"That's right," Mr. Rollins said. "Now, Billy, you stop picking at Juliet."

"And, Juliet, you stop picking at Billy," Mr. Jones said. "That's not a bear track anyway. I don't know what it is, but it's not that."

With a lot of grumbling under his breath, Billy turned away and began to roll up his sleeping bag. "It wasn't me, Dad," he said. "Honest. Juliet's picking on me."

"Then just ignore her. Let's just have fun while we're out here," Mr. Rollins said. "It's the first time we've done anything together in a long time, and I don't want to have it spoiled."

After the bear print business was settled, the morning went fairly well.

Mr. Jones announced, "Today Amos is going to give us a lesson in plants, if he's willing. All right, Amos?"

"If you say so, Mr. Jones."

"Don't load us down with too much stuff," Joe said. "I know too much already. It's making me so heavy I can hardly walk. Juliet, maybe you ought to carry my pack. With all this learning in my head, it's just awful hard."

That brought a laugh from everybody. His father said, "I think you have a little room left, say, for math."

"Don't talk about math, Dad. Not out here.

When you're out in the woods, math doesn't exist. It only exists inside houses and schools and places."

"Where'd you get that idea?"

"Oh, I've always thought that, Dad!" Joe teased. "I think some schoolteacher a long time ago needed a job. So he said, 'I'm going to make up a subject to teach. I'll make up all kinds of rules, and then I'll get a job teaching it.'"

Flash and Chili groaned. They both knew how much Joe hated math.

"It you'd just stop hating math so much and study it," Juliet said, "it would be easier!"

"Most of the subjects I don't like, somebody just made them up," Joe declared grandly.

"We'll argue that when we get back into the classroom," Mr. Jones said. "But for now, Amos, don't burden Joe down too much. Just give us one or two samples of what you've learned about wild plants."

Amos said he would, and ten minutes later he stopped the group and said, "There's a plant everybody ought to know." He pointed to some large plants, then pulled up one. "See these greenish white flowers and these red berries? This is a very important plant."

"What is it?" Juliet asked.

"It's called ginseng."

"I've heard about that," Joe said. "But where did I hear about it? Now let me see."

"It's pretty valuable stuff."

"Why is it valuable?" Jenny asked.

"A lot of people use it for medicine. You can find it in grocery stores sometimes."

"Hey, that's where I saw it!" Joe snapped his fingers. He looked around at the ginseng plants. "There are a lot of them growing here. If the stores buy them, let's pull up a bunch and take them back and sell them."

"No, no," his dad said. "Not on this outing. We can't be bothered with that. Besides, I'm not even sure that the grocery stores would buy them. But it's nice to know things like this."

From time to time Amos stopped and told them the names of different plants, until Joe finally said, "My head's getting too full. Back off, Amos. I don't want to learn too much."

Juliet thought all this was a great deal of fun. She really admired Amos for knowing so much about plants.

And then, right in the middle of things, Jenny asked, "Juliet, what do you think happened to those cups?"

"I don't know, but people are getting suspicious of *me*."

"Oh no. Why should they?"

"I just think they are." Juliet was truly disturbed. "Anyway, I don't think a bear made that track, and tonight we're going to have to stay awake. Both of us. This trip will soon be over, and we won't have any more chances to catch whoever it is that's doing this."

95

"We can take turns," Jenny said. "You take the first watch, and I'll take the second. That's what they always do in the movies."

"That's what we'll do, and we'll catch whoever it is that's pulling this off."

"I can't imagine who it is, can you?"

"No, I really can't. Well . . . I do have a suspicion."

"Really? Who do you think it is?"

"I can't tell. Not now, at least. I don't have enough to go on, but I've got a vague idea of who it might be because . . . Anyway we'll stay up tonight, and maybe we'll catch him."

Sounds in the Night

The stream along the trail widened until finally it ran into a large pond, and that gave the boys and girls something special to do.

"We're going to go exploring," Joe announced. "We're going all the way around this pond."

"Yeah!" Chili agreed. "What's the good of being in the wilderness if you can't explore?"

Flash said he would stay where he was and do some fishing.

"I think we'll just look for stuff around here," Juliet said. She did not want to admit it, but she was tired, and she suspected that the other girls were too.

Billy Rollins wasn't fooled. "I knew you girls couldn't make it. I'm surprised you got this far. Come on, guys. Let's leave these weaklings here."

As soon as they were gone, Flash started to fish, and the girls began to walk along the pond. The men were setting up the tents this time, and Juliet said, "I'm glad we'll get to sleep inside. It looks like it might rain again."

Jenny checked the sky, too. It was a little overcast. She said, "I hope it doesn't. I'd like for us to get back without any more bad weather."

"I know what we can do," Delores said. "Let's see if we can find any of those important plants Amos has been teaching us about."

"We can try," Juliet said. "If we don't find any plants to eat, maybe we can find some that are pretty. I love wildflowers."

The girls wandered on. Soon Juliet was saying, "I know this one. It's what Amos called Dutchman's-breeches."

"Such a funny name," Jenny said. "But it is a beautiful little plant." She picked one. It was fragile and tiny with a white blossom. "Let's make a bouquet out of all the different kinds of flowers that we find."

"All right. I'd like to have something pretty around."

"Oh, here's something pretty, but I don't know what it is," Delores said.

"I do. That's a violet."

"I thought violets were purple."

"They are usually, but this kind is white. Don't you remember? Amos told us about that. I think he said it was a Canadian violet."

The girls soon had gathered enough flowers for two bouquets. "We don't have anything to put them in," Juliet said. "They'll wilt pretty fast."

"I know," Jenny said. "But it's fun to collect them anyway."

Then Juliet saw some gray squirrels high in a grove of towering oaks. "Hello," she called. "You'd better stay away, or the boys will trap you, and we'll be having you for supper."

The squirrels chattered at her angrily.

"They don't like us being here."

"Well, this is their home, I guess," Jenny said.

As they wandered on, they saw many signs of deer going to the little lake. Their tracks were everywhere.

"I don't see any bear tracks though," Delores said, sounding relieved. "That's good. I'd hate to meet a bear."

"So would I. Or a mountain lion." Juliet shivered. "I'm glad there's nothing like that around here. Imagine meeting a lion out in the woods with no place to hide."

The morning wore on, and the girls went back.

The boys showed up soon afterward. Billy trailed in last, breathing hard. He said, "We went around the whole pond!"

"See any bears?" Juliet looked at him directly.

Billy must have known she was referring to his remarks the previous day. "No, we didn't see any, but there wasn't anybody out there to make bear tracks, either."

"Now, don't you two start picking on each other," Jenny said. "There's no point in it."

"That's right," Juliet said quickly. She had resolved to try to get along with Billy a little better. She said, "Here, Billy, we found some flowers. You boys can have this bouquet."

Billy looked surprised and a little embarrassed. He stood looking down at the flowers she'd thrust into his hand. Then he said gruffly, "Well . . . thanks."

"You're welcome."

"I don't know what a guy's supposed to do with flowers out here, though."

"I know. They'll be fading soon, but they are pretty, aren't they?"

"Uh . . . yeah, they're kind of pretty," Billy said. He looked at her and said again, "Well, thanks."

After he left, Jenny laughed. "Billy doesn't know what to do when someone does something nice for him."

"I've got the idea that underneath that obnoxious outside, he's not so bad," Juliet said.

"Well, he keeps the good part hidden pretty well," Delores said.

All afternoon the homeschoolers wandered over the countryside, staying close to the trail as their group leaders told them to. Juliet and a few others were back at camp when Chili returned from exploring and said, "Anybody want to come and see what I found?"

"I hope it's worth all this trouble," Billy grumbled as they followed him down the trail.

"It is. Wait till you see," Chili said.

He led them to a rocky shelf where water was pouring out of a small hole.

"Is that what you brought us here to see? A spring?"

"Not just a spring," Chili said. "Feel it."

Juliet was standing closest. She put her hand into the water and jerked it back. "Why, it's hot!"

"Yeah, a hot spring," Chili said. "I've never even seen one before."

"I have—in Yellowstone National Park," Jack said. "There are lots of them there."

"There are some in Hot Springs, Arkansas, too," Delores said. "We were there one time."

"How can the water be hot when the weather is cold?" Joe puzzled.

"I know," Daniel said. "I heard it comes from way down deep where it's much hotter." He felt the water again. "This is so warm you could take a bath in it."

"Not me," Joe said. "I'm off baths until further notice."

Juliet was thinking, *Taking a bath here*

*would be nice, but I don't have any soap or towel
—or privacy—so I guess I'll just have to wait.*

When they got back to the campsite, everybody organized a ball game and played until suppertime.

It was a good supper. Mr. Tanner had gone hunting and came back with a sackful of birds.

"What are they?" Juliet asked.

"They're quail. Best eating bird there is. A lot like chicken, only better."

The roasted quail did turn out to be excellent. There was not quite enough to satisfy everybody, but everyone got some.

Juliet ate hers greedily. "It's so good, Mr. Tanner. It's too bad they're not as big as chickens."

He chuckled. "It would take chicken-size quail to fill up this gang."

They sat around the campfire, as usual, while it grew dark.

"Tonight I'd like each of us to tell what this trip has meant to us," Mr. Jones said. "Who wants to be first?"

There was total silence. The boys and girls all seemed a little embarrassed.

Finally Joe spoke up, "It's meant a lot to me, Dad. And I want to thank you and the rest of the Support Group for giving us an outing like this. It's been a great time."

Then, to Juliet's surprise, Billy Rollins said,

"Well, there's been some trouble, but it's been good for me to spend some time with my dad."

Mr. Rollins looked a little sheepish. "It won't be the last time, Billy," he promised. "This trip has been good for me too. We'll be doing things like this again."

Around the circle they went, and everybody had something to say. Juliet was next to last.

She said, "I want to specially thank all you who came to chaperone us. And I've learned a lot. Amos has taught us a lot about plants, and I know I'll never forget that. Then, it's made me appreciate the things I take for granted at home."

"Yeah, like not having to take baths," Joe broke in.

Even Juliet laughed at that. She said, "We don't agree on taking baths, but I think doing without things will make me appreciate how nice the things are that we have at home."

Last of all, Jenny said, "I'm grateful to the Lord for letting us spend this time together, and I don't want to forget to thank Him for it."

Mr. Jones said, "It's been good to hear from all of you. Now let's have a prayer before we go to bed." They all bowed their heads, and he prayed, "Lord, we thank You for this time that we have had out in Your wonderful world. You are the creator of all of this that we see, and Your world is beautiful. We thank You for the time that we've had together."

When he lifted his head, he said, "We've got an early start in the morning, and I think it's time to hit the sack."

Juliet, Delores, and Jenny were soon in their sleeping bags in their tent. Outside, the fire still crackled. The men sat up for a short time talking and drinking coffee, but finally they went to bed, too.

Juliet and Jenny had agreed to take turns watching, but Juliet saw that Jenny dropped off to sleep at once. *I guess it's my turn first, then,* she thought. She was determined to stay awake this time.

From time to time Too Smart Jones had to pinch herself, but she did manage to keep her eyes open. She entertained herself by listening to the night sounds. There was the crackling fire and the popping of the wood as it sent off yellow sparks. Every so often the logs would settle, making a hissing sound. Far off, some dogs were barking. She heard an owl calling, "Whoo—whoo!" just overhead.

Juliet grew very sleepy. She found her eyes almost impossible to keep open. She clutched her sleeping bag tightly around her, determined that even though she closed her eyes she would not go to sleep. And then something scratched on the side of the tent.

Instantly she stiffened.

What was that? she thought fearfully. Cautiously she lifted her head.

Something *was* scratching on their tent! She saw what looked like a long finger, poking and scraping just above her head. It would touch one spot, disappear, then appear somewhere else.

Juliet started to get up. "Who's there?" She had some trouble getting out of her sleeping bag. By the time she did, Jenny and Delores were scrambling out, too. They began screaming.

"Stop yelling!" she said. "You'll scare everybody to death."

"What's going on in here?" Juliet's dad was at their tent door with a flashlight.

"I think there was a wild animal, Dad. I could see it touching the tent."

Mr. Jones gave his daughter a hard look. "All right," he said, "we'll check."

He made a circle of the tent while the girls stood outside waiting. Then he came back, shaking his head. "There's nothing here. You've let your imagination run away with you, Juliet. Or you were dreaming."

"Dad, I know I saw something, and I heard it, too! It was scratching."

"Juliet, if there was anything, it was probably just the breeze. Or maybe it was a tree branch scratching against the top."

"That's what it was," Jenny said. "See? This branch is touching the top of our tent right now. That's all you heard."

"All of you go on back to bed. Now! And, Juliet, try to keep your imagination under control. *Go to sleep!*"

"All right, Dad."

The girls went back inside, and Delores said, "He was a little mad, wasn't he?"

"No, he wasn't mad." Juliet frowned. "He was just upset."

Again the camp grew quiet, but Juliet did not go to sleep. *I'm sure I heard something,* she thought. *I know I saw something at the top of the tent. And it wasn't a branch.*

And then she heard something hissing. *Snakes hiss,* she thought. *I wonder if it could be a snake out there.*

If she had not been so sleepy, she would have remembered that snakes were not out at that time of the year. But she was not thinking clearly. She went outside again and started looking around. But she found no snakes.

She turned around to see Jenny standing behind her.

"What is it this time?" Jenny asked.

"I thought I heard something."

"Heard what?"

"Well, it sounded like a snake."

"Ooh, a snake! I can't stand snakes!"

"Hush! Don't wake up Dad again. He's upset enough."

"I can't go to sleep with snakes around."

"Oh, it wasn't a snake! I should have

known better," Juliet said, remembering. "It's too cold for snakes. Probably just the wind. Let's go back to bed."

They did.

"Look at Delores," Juliet whispered. "She hasn't even turned over with all this racket we're making."

She lay still in her sleeping bag. More than once she heard rustling in the fallen leaves outside, but she did not want to upset her father again. She clenched her teeth and kept her eyes wide open.

Every time a new sound came, she wanted to get up and investigate, but she didn't. She thought, *I can't go to sleep now, and I can't go out to look around, either. Dad would be upset. He thinks it's all my imagination.*

The night wore on, the campfire finally died down, and Juliet got drowsy. She thought about waking Jenny to ask her to take a watch, but Jenny was sound asleep.

Dad was probably right. It was probably my own imagination. I've got too much of that, she thought sleepily. *I'm going to have to keep it down.* She drifted off and knew nothing more until daylight the next morning.

The Toothbrush

Juliet felt someone's hand on her shoulder, but she was so tired she could not come out of sleep.

"Let me alone," she moaned.

"Come on, Juliet. Time to get up."

Rolling over, she shielded her eyes, for the sun was streaming through the tent flap. She closed them for a moment, then sat up. Her father was looking in, and she saw that Delores and Jenny were already gone. "What is it, Dad?" she mumbled.

"You can't sleep all day," he said cheerfully. "Everybody else has been up for a long time. Here. I saved you some breakfast."

"What time is it?"

"It's after nine o'clock. We let everybody sleep late this morning." Her father looked at her carefully. "You've got dark shadows under your eyes. You look like you don't feel well."

"I feel all right."

"Are you sure?"

"I'm sure, Dad. I guess I'm just tired."

"OK, then. You'd better eat something. It's going to be a busy day."

"Thanks, Dad."

Juliet ate the granola bar without much appetite. There was some leftover quail, and she ate that too. Her dad had also brought her a cup of hot chocolate, which was *very* good.

"Hey, you're a real sleepyhead!"

Juliet looked up to see Chili squatting by the tent flap. "I thought you had died. Everybody else has been up for hours."

"I was just tired."

He nodded. "Everybody's a little tired. Surviving in the wilderness is pretty rough."

Juliet swallowed the last of the chocolate. "Yes, but it's been fun. Anyway, I'll be glad to get home and get rested up."

"How come you're so tired this morning?"

"Well, I tried to stay awake as long as I could."

"Stay awake!" He laughed. "What did you want to do that for? Most of us want to sleep as much as we can."

"I thought I might catch the thief."

Chili looked at her, his eyebrows going up.

"Oh, you mean whoever took the stuff that's missing."

"Sure, that's who I mean. Who did you think I meant?"

"Oh, I don't know," Chili said. "Did you stay up all night?"

"I tried to, but I couldn't do it."

"Anyhow, we're almost ready to go home now. I don't guess you have to worry about anybody taking anything else."

Juliet shook her head. "I just hate to have a mystery like this go unsolved. It's driving me crazy."

"You'll figure it out someday," Chili said with a little smile. "You always do. Just another easy mystery for Too Smart Jones to solve."

"Come on, Chili. *Don't* call me that."

"Oops, sorry. I forgot again. You don't like that name. Well, you'd better come out of there. We're going to be moving on pretty soon. Lots of fun things to do today."

"I'm coming."

Juliet straightened her clothes and went to wash her face. Back in the tent she started to brush her hair. When she was almost through, Delores came in. "Hello. I was afraid you were sick."

"Everybody's worried about me. Nope, I'm all right. Just tired."

Jenny came in, too. "We didn't want to

111

bother you getting our toothbrushes out, but I need mine now."

"So do I," Delores said.

The two girls rummaged through their knapsacks, and Jenny found her toothbrush at once. "Hurry up, Delores!" she said.

"I'm going as fast as I can!" Delores protested.

Juliet found her own toothbrush and toothpaste. "Let's go down to the stream. My teeth feel all gritty."

Delores said, "My toothbrush is gone!"

"It can't be gone," Juliet told her. "You put it back last night after we brushed our teeth. I saw you do it."

"I put it right on top where I could get it early this morning. I didn't put it inside."

"Then you probably knocked it off."

Delores kept her knapsack right by the opening of the tent, because there was not much room inside. She'd claimed she needed all the room she could get. She scrambled around now, moving the knapsack and looking everywhere. Then she looked up at them, big-eyed. "Somebody's stolen it."

Jenny stared back at her. "Why would anyone steal your *toothbrush?*"

"Taking it wouldn't have been too hard," Juliet said. "You two slept like you were dead."

"But didn't *you* stay awake?" Jenny asked.

"I was going to. If you remember," Juliet said, "we were going to take turns."

"Oh, I'm sorry, Juliet!" Jenny said. "I was just so sleepy. You should have wakened me."

"You were sleeping so good I didn't want to. I thought I could make it all night, but I didn't."

The three girls looked at each other.

Delores finally said, "Imagine. That's some nerve, stealing my *toothbrush!* What am I supposed to do about my teeth now? My teeth will feel dirty all day long!"

"No, they won't," Jenny said. "I brought two toothbrushes, just in case." She fished in her knapsack. "Here. You can have my extra."

"Oh, thanks, Jenny! I can't stand not brushing my teeth in the morning. But who would want to steal a *toothbrush?*"

The tents were down, and everybody seemed ready to go. As the girls joined the crowd, Flash Gordon was declaring, "I guess we had one night without anything being stolen."

"No, we didn't," Delores announced.

"What are you talking about?" her brother piped up. "What's missing now?"

"My toothbrush!" Delores said.

"Your toothbrush! Good grief," Joe said. "How could you lose your toothbrush?"

"I didn't lose it! Somebody took it!"

"You kept it in your knapsack, didn't you? Nobody could have crawled into your tent and gone through your knapsack and stolen your toothbrush without somebody waking up!" Samuel protested.

"I always keep my knapsack by the opening of the tent, and I put the toothbrush right on top so I could find it this morning."

"Then you probably just knocked it off. Take another look," Billy said in disgust.

"No, it's gone. I've looked everywhere."

Mr. Tanner glanced over at Mr. Jones, and Mr. Jones glanced over at Mr. Tanner.

"Boys and girls," Juliet's dad said, "that's been the worst part of this whole trip—things missing. Now, kids, I want to know the truth. Has anyone been just playing around?"

All of the youngsters denied it.

Chili came back about then, carrying a bucket of water to pour over the campfire. He said, "Great day for camping out." Then he looked around at the serious faces. "What's everybody so glum about?"

"Somebody stole my toothbrush!" Delores said.

"How could that be?"

Jenny went over the whole story again.

Mr. Jones said, "Well, we've about talked this thing to death. Let's forget about it for the time being. After all, it's only a toothbrush this time. Nothing really valuable."

"My canteen was valuable!" Billy protested.

114

"I've told you I'm going to get you a better canteen."

"But I liked *that* one."

"Son, let's just forget it for right now."

"I think that's a good idea," Mr. Jones said. "The thing is not to let it spoil our wilderness trip. Let's just have fun today and try to learn as much as we can. OK?"

Everybody agreed, and shortly afterward the group began their hike down the river. Up ahead, Chili called out, "Come on! No laggers now!"

Juliet marched along beside Joe. Close behind them were their new friends, Daniel and Kelsey.

Juliet thought, *I wonder if it could be Kelsey or Daniel taking things. We don't know much about them, and I'd hate to think it was any of my old friends.*

But when Daniel and Kelsey asked her about the missing toothbrush, she found herself telling them about last night. "I heard all kinds of funny sounds," she said. "Some of them I didn't even recognize."

"That's the way it is in the woods," Daniel said. As usual, he was wearing his fatigues and looked much like a soldier.

"I guess so," Juliet said, "but *someone* took that toothbrush."

"Have you ever had anything like this happen before, Juliet?" Kelsey asked. She came up beside Juliet. "They say you're great at solving mysteries."

"She sure hasn't solved this one." Billy was behind them now. "Doesn't look like you're going to, does it, Too Smart?"

Juliet did not answer.

At break time, she went off by herself and took her journal from her backpack. She read the notes that she had made but could make nothing out of them. She read them over and over again.

She tried to think of who in the world could be taking things and *why*. This was different from the bicycle mystery. The bicycles had been stolen by thieves who intended to sell them. But many of the things that were missing here were not really valuable.

The rest of the day on the trail, she could not put the matter out of her mind. "I don't know who's doing this, but I'm beginning to have an idea . . ."

"What are you thinking about so seriously, Juliet?"

Juliet looked up to see her father coming up beside her.

"Oh, nothing much, Dad!"

"Now, I know you better than that. You've got that look in your eye."

"What kind of look?"

"That I'm-going-to-solve-this-mystery look."

116

She laughed. "You know me pretty well, Dad." She took his hand and held onto it. "It bothers me that all these things were taken— and we don't know who or why."

"It bothers me too. I'd hate to think that one of our kids has become a thief. Have you got any ideas?"

"Just one. But I can't tell you."

"Oh, you're withholding information?"

"Well, I might not be right, and it wouldn't be good for me to tell you unless I was absolutely sure."

Mr. Jones smiled. "I'm glad to hear you say that, Juliet. We never want to make any accusation until we're absolutely sure."

Juliet walked along beside her father, her hand warm in his. She wanted to tell him what she suspected, but now he had said what she had felt all along. It was never good to say anything accusing about another person unless there was evidence.

She kept trying to put the mystery together as they tramped along, but she didn't get far with it. *We'll soon be home,* she said to herself, *and then all this will be over. But, somehow or other, I'll figure it out before we get back.*

The Hat

This is our last day in the wilderness," Juliet said with a sigh.

Jenny was munching on a handful of trail mix. Juliet hated trail mix, but Jenny seemed to love it.

"I think it's been great," Jenny said. She chewed thoughtfully, then said, "I'm looking forward to our trip down the river."

"Me too," Juliet said. "I've never been in a canoe before. I hear they're awfully easy to tip over."

"Well, there'll be life jackets for everyone, and we'll have a leader in every canoe. So I guess we'll be all right." She offered the bag of trail mix to Juliet. "Have some."

"No, thanks. I can't stand that stuff. Oh, what I wouldn't give for a Snickers bar!"

Jenny laughed and took another mouthful. "You're just spoiled. That's what you are."

"I suppose so. Just imagine being able to go to the refrigerator and get some ice cream and pour chocolate syrup over the top . . ."

"Your mother lets you do that any time you want to?"

"No way," Juliet said. "But I get more ice cream and chocolate syrup at home than I've had out here this week! This wilderness trip has really made me appreciate things more."

"I was reading about some of the pioneers—how hungry they got for sweet things."

"That's right. They didn't have candy bars to carry with them then."

"And the book said they really had a good time when they found a bee tree full of honey. The men would go out and smoke it and then cut it down. But they still got a lot of stings."

"I wouldn't mind having some honey right now, but I wouldn't want to get stung for it."

Jenny looked around. "Where have all the boys gone?"

"Oh, Mr. Harris and my dad took them out hunting. Mr. Harris had his bow and arrow, and he was going to try to kill a wild turkey."

"I doubt if he'll do it, though," Jenny said.

"Why do you doubt it?"

"Because I heard him say that wild turkeys are very shy."

"What's that got to do with it?"

"Can you imagine trying to sneak up on *anything* with that bunch of boys along? They make more racket than a herd of wild elephants."

Juliet giggled. "How many herds of wild elephants have you heard?"

"Not many. But you know how noisy they are. They'll be laughing and giggling, and Mr. Harris will be lucky if he gets within a mile of a turkey."

Jenny was mistaken, however. Two hours later the hunters came back, and Mr. Harris was holding a wild turkey high in the air.

"Look what we got!" All the boys were shouting.

"We?" Joe said to Samuel, who was hollering loudest. "What do you mean 'we'?"

"We all went, didn't we?" Samuel grinned broadly. "Mr. Harris actually brought him down, but I could have."

Juliet soon learned that all the boys had had a chance to take shots with the bow, but none of their arrows came anywhere close.

"Bow and arrow's just not my game," Joe sniffed. "Now if I'd had a shotgun, I bet you I could have got one."

"I'm glad we got this bird," Mr. Harris said. "Let's get him cleaned. Then we'll have a pre-Thanksgiving turkey dinner."

Juliet helped to pluck the feathers from the turkey. It was a messy job, she thought. She had never tried to pluck a bird before. She said, "I'd hate to have to pluck every turkey and chicken I ate. This is awful!"

Mr. Harris finished cleaning the turkey, and before long it was roasting over the fire.

While the bird was cooking, the youngsters went exploring around the campsite. Amos showed them some more wildflowers and plants. Some of the boys went fishing. By the time they came back, everyone claimed to be half-starved.

"Look at that turkey!" Joe breathed. "I could eat the whole thing all by myself."

"You won't get the chance," Daniel Saville said. "I'm gonna eat my share of it."

The turkey turned out to be tougher and drier than turkeys from the supermarket, and Mr. Harris explained. "The turkeys you get in the store never get any exercise. They're kept in large pens, and they're fed foods that make them fat so they'll weigh more. These fellows—" he carved another slice of meat "—they have to scratch for a living, so they're strong and muscular."

Juliet had gotten one of the legs, and she was enjoying it thoroughly. She sprinkled more salt over it and said, "It tastes good to me. I just wish he'd had *four* legs."

"A four-legged turkey." Billy laughed. "That would be something to see."

"Maybe you ought to try breeding a special turkey," Joe said. "The Too Smart Jones four-legged turkey. You'd make a fortune."

Juliet let them tease. She and the other girls had made biscuits, using flour that Mr. Harris had brought in his provisions. They had baked them on flat stones in front of the fire. She picked up one and said, "These aren't as good as Mom's."

"You know what they called this sort of thing during the Revolutionary War?" Mr. Harris asked.

"No, what?" Joe wanted to know.

"They called them fire cakes. Many times the soldiers had only a little flour, so they would mix it with water and then toast the dough on their bayonets—or sometimes on hot rocks before the fire, like we did. So they called them fire cakes."

"Doesn't sound like much to eat. Just flour-and-water biscuits,"

"It wasn't. Those soldiers had a rough time."

Then Juliet said, "Now we have a surprise. Here's dessert."

"Looks just like more biscuits to me," Joe said, taking one of them.

"Well, bite into it, and you'll find it's different." Juliet grinned at Jenny.

Joe took a bite, and his eyes opened with surprise. "Hey, this is sweet!"

"Sure it is. Look at it. It's got berries inside. Blueberries—we think," Jenny said.

Everyone began scrambling for a dessert biscuit.

And then Joe said, "You mean you don't know what kind of berries these are?"

"We didn't at the time. And Amos wasn't there right then to tell us."

"I hope they're not poison," Amos said innocently.

"Poison!" Billy Rollins stared at his biscuit, and his face turned pale. "They might be poison?"

Amos turned away so that Billy could not see his smile. "Plenty of poison berries out here. We'll just hope for the best. You've had two already, Billy, so you'll be the first to go."

Billy abruptly put down his biscuit. "I'm not eating any more of these!" he declared.

Amos reached over and picked it up. "Then I'll finish it off. If it hasn't killed you yet, it won't do me any harm."

The berry biscuits were soon all gone, and then Billy realized he had been tricked. "You stole my biscuit, Amos!"

"I didn't steal it. You said you weren't going to eat it. I wasn't about to let it go to waste."

A lot of laughter went around, but Juliet said, "Don't worry, Billy. I saved a couple for later. Here, you can have one of them."

Billy took it but looked suspicious. "Why are you being so nice to me?"

"I'm naturally nice," Juliet teased. "You just haven't noticed."

Billy seemed not to know exactly how to handle that. However, he ate the biscuit, as Mr. Jones used the last of the chocolate to make them one last hot drink.

Later, as they sat about the campfire, Joe said, "We'd better have some good stories. This is our last night out."

"I'm sorry it's all over," Samuel said. "It'll be dull going home after this."

"Oh, I don't know," Chili said. "We always find lots to do. The trip's been exciting though. Especially the mystery of who's been taking people's stuff."

"I wish you hadn't brought that up, Chili," Flash said. "I'm trying to forget it."

"Well, *you* haven't lost anything!" Billy protested.

"No, I haven't, but other people have. I think it's too bad."

Chili shrugged his shoulders. "Oh, well. Everything will probably turn up."

Juliet was depressed by the mention of the stolen articles. Although there was a lot of singing and games and storytelling around the campfire, she could not enthusiastically take part in anything.

Later, as she crawled into her sleeping bag, Juliet saw Jenny putting her toothbrush safely down in the depths of her knapsack.

"I'll see he won't get that," Juliet said. "Who-ever's taking things."

"He sure won't," Jenny said. "It's the last toothbrush on the place, and I'm not going to lose it."

"You'd have another one tomorrow," Delores said. "You'll be home. But just to be sure, maybe we ought to put our knapsacks down at the other end of the tent. Away from the door."

Juliet and Jenny thought this was a good idea.

"I'll be glad to get home again," Delores said with a sigh.

"Me too. I miss Mom's cooking," Juliet said.

"And I miss my grandmother's. What I wouldn't give for a good enchilada with lots of hot pepper sauce."

"The next time we go camping, we'll have to take along some hot pepper sauce. We could use some on turkey or fish or whatever."

"That would be nice," Delores said.

It was a beautiful night. Juliet lay listening as Delores and Jenny talked about what had happened that day. Outside, the leaders talked as they drank coffee around the fire. Finally their voices died down, and apparently every-one went to sleep.

Juliet was still determined to solve the mystery of the missing items. She had placed her sleeping bag so that her head was at the tent opening. From there she could see some of the stars. She picked out the Big Dipper and remembered what her father had said: "To find the North Star, you find the outside of the cup of the Dipper. Those two stars point right to the north, so if you just draw an imaginary line from them, you'll find the brightest star all by itself. That's Polaris."

Juliet did find the bright star, and she knew she had found the very star that had guided so many sailors for so many hundreds and maybe thousands of years. *It never changes,* she thought. *God keeps it right there in the same place.*

That was almost her last waking thought.

Too Smart Jones soon found herself dreaming. It was a fine dream, too. She dreamed of Boots, her cat, with his white feet and bright green eyes. She thought he was pouncing on her in bed. She tried to catch him, but he was too quick for her.

Then the dream changed. Now she and Boots were running through a field of beautiful wildflowers—yellow, blue, and red. She could smell their fragrance, and overhead the sun was bright. It was a huge yellow disk that shed its warm beams down upon the meadow where they ran. She could hear music playing somewhere far away. It was the most beautiful music she had ever heard.

Juliet knew that she was just dreaming.

Usually, when she dreamed, she would awaken with a shock to find she was back in the real world. But even as she ran through the wildflowers, she was thinking, *This is all a dream. Sometime I'm going to wake up.*

She did wake up—abruptly—when a noise sounded right outside the tent. Her eyes flew open, and she thought, *Somebody's tripped over something.*

She listened. Sure enough, it sounded as if someone was moving around on the ground. Maybe getting up.

Then she thought, *Oh, it's just Dad or one of the other men checking on us.* Still, when she looked at her watch, she saw it was almost two o'clock in the morning.

They wouldn't be up that late. It's got to be something else.

Cautiously she lifted her head. She heard again the sound of something moving. She unzipped her bag and got out.

Now the sound was coming from across the campsite. Juliet peered out. The fire had died down and gave very little light. Overhead, however, the moon was bright.

Something's moving over there. It's headed for those trees along the trail.

Juliet watched for a long time. *Was* something there? *Maybe I was just imagining I saw something moving,* she thought. *Maybe the wind is blowing those bushes around.*

For some time she sat there without seeing anything else. She looked again at her watch. *Who in their right mind would be out at two-thirty in the morning just to play a trick? We had too hard a day. Nobody would be playing jokes this time of night.*

Then Juliet took out her journal and her penlight. She wrote what had happened that day. The other girls were sleeping so soundly they were not disturbed at all.

Then she turned off the penlight and looked out the tent flap again. *I still think I see something there, but it's not moving,* she thought. *It's just my wild imagination. Every night I've heard or seen something. I've got to learn to control my imagination.*

Juliet slept fitfully until the morning sunlight struck her face. She heard people moving around and talking. She noticed that the two other girls were up and gone. And then she heard Joe yelling.

Sticking her head out the tent door, she said, "Joe Jones, what are you yelling about?"

Joe stomped toward her. His face was wearing an awful frown. *"Somebody stole my hat!"*

"Stole your hat?"

"Yeah, my favorite hat!"

Juliet pulled on her boots and went out.

Others began to gather around, and Joe eyed them suspiciously. "OK, any of you guys playing tricks, you'd better give me my hat. That's enough of this. It's not funny anymore."

Everyone denied taking his hat.

But Joe said, "I want everybody's pack turned upside down. That hat's got to be somewhere!"

Nothing else would satisfy him, so they all dutifully unpacked their backpacks. Of course, they found nothing, and Joe was smoldering.

Mr. Harris came over to Juliet. "I'm beginning to think you may have the right idea after all. Somebody is deliberately doing this."

Juliet said, "I still don't want to accuse anybody, Mr. Harris. I don't really have any evidence. Just some . . . ideas."

Billy Rollins was standing so close that he heard. "What's that about evidence?" he asked.

"Oh, I've just been keeping notes on what's been happening, Billy," Juliet answered hastily.

"If you've got any evidence, let's have it."

"Nothing like that," Juliet said. "I've just got a . . . a suspicion."

"Well, I've got my suspicions, too. What's yours?"

"I really can't say yet. It wouldn't be fair. I just have to be quite sure."

"What you mean is Too Smart Jones is foiled again!" Billy clomped off.

The campers pulled out shortly after that and headed toward the point where the canoes were waiting.

* * *

As they hiked along, Juliet talked to Jenny about the mystery. "It's really gotten the best of me," she said. "I guess it's good for my pride, though. I was beginning to think I could solve any mystery, and now it looks like here's one I can't."

"Oh, we'll find out someday, maybe. Or maybe not," Jenny said, not very encouragingly.

The thought of not solving a mystery troubled Juliet a great deal. She enjoyed hiking through the beautiful woods, but all the time she was thinking, *Somehow I've got to get to the bottom of this.* One thought kept coming to her, and she kept pushing it away. On one of their breaks, she took out her notebook and made a few notes.

"What are you writing down?" Joe asked.

"Oh, nothing much. Just stuff."

Joe eyed her. "I know you, Juliet," he said. "You're up to something. What is it?"

"Nothing. I just had a few thoughts I wanted to write down. It's kind of like a journal."

"Well, keep me out of it. I don't want to star in your journal."

"All right, Joe. I'll keep you out of it."

Juliet said no more, but she kept thinking. From time to time she would write. At last she put the journal away and sighed. *Well, that's*

131

the best I can come up with, she thought. She would give all her attention to hiking to where the canoes waited.

Home Again

Joe looked up at the tall trees that met above the trail. "You know what, Dad?" he said quietly. "I've had more fun on this outing than most any trip in my whole life."

Mr. Jones smiled down at him. "And so have I."

"Have you really?"

"Sure."

"I've learned so much. I'm going to use what I've learned every chance I get, too." Joe thought for a moment. "Of course, it hasn't been *all* fun. Somebody taking my favorite hat—that wasn't fun."

"We've never gotten to the bottom of that one," his dad said. "I don't understand any of it, but everything else has been good."

Far back in the line of walkers, Kelsey Saville was holding the tiny bird that she had found. She had hand-fed it and coddled it like a baby. Kelsey said, "See, it's able to move that wing now. I'll bet it can fly."

"You think it'd be safe to let it go?"

"As safe as it ever is for a little bird," Kelsey said. "Birds have a hard time. Especially at first. There are so many dangers." She cooed at it. "Poor little bird. It's time to let you go."

The girls made a ceremony out of taking the bandage off the bird's wing. Kelsey opened her palm. And the little bird began to flap its wings.

"Look, he *can* fly!"

It appeared the bird could fly for short distances for it fluttered to a bush. As it flew off again, they all called after it, "Good-bye, birdie! Good-bye!"

"You did a good job, Kelsey," Juliet said. "It was kind of you to take care of that little bird."

Kelsey's brother grinned. "She takes in all kinds of animals. We had a baby coon for a while. We tried to take him back to the woods, and he wouldn't go for a long time. Finally he did, though."

About an hour after this, they reached the river. There the canoes were waiting. They had been brought in by some of the other fathers on pickup trucks.

"How many of you have never ridden in a canoe?" Mr. Jones asked. He looked at the hands. "Well, those of you who haven't must remember one important thing. Canoes tip over very easily."

"That's right," Mr. Tanner added. "Every one of you has to wear a life jacket. You'll find them in the bottom of the canoes."

"Oh, I can swim!" Billy protested.

"No exceptions!" Mr. Tanner said. "Everybody wears a life jacket."

The men placed Flash and his fold-up wheelchair in the biggest canoe.

Juliet found herself assigned to the canoe with Chili and her father. When they had their life jackets on and were ready to sit down, Chili said, "Let me ride in the front."

Juliet laughed at him. "You always have to be in front."

"I guess so. I just like to be up there. Doesn't ever do any good to come in second."

"You've had a real good time on this trip, haven't you?" Juliet asked him.

"Best time in my whole life. My dad says now he's found out how much fun this is, we're going to do it again. You've had a good time, too?"

"Oh, yes!"

"Even if you didn't get the mystery solved?" he asked curiously.

Juliet smiled a little smile and shrugged her shoulders. "Well, you can't win 'em all."

They had no time for further talk because

the canoes were all loaded and Mr. Jones was asking, "Everyone ready?"

"Yes!" everybody hollered.

"Then, let's go." He added to Juliet and Chili, "You two steady up now." He pushed their canoe out into the water and then leaped into it at the last moment. It rocked wildly, and Juliet grabbed for the sides.

"It's OK," her dad assured her. "Here we go. You paddle on the right, Juliet. You on the left, Chili. I'll do the steering from back here."

And they headed downstream. The river flowed fairly slowly, but with three paddling in each canoe they made good time. They passed beneath cliffs that rose high over them, and once Chili said, "Look, there's an otter!"

Juliet started to stand up to look, but her father said quickly, "Sit down! You *never* stand up in a canoe, Juliet."

"Sorry, Dad. I forgot."

But there were other things to see, and Juliet thought it was a beautiful trip.

When they had traveled for an hour, Mr. Jones guided the canoes toward a sand bar. "All out. Time for snacks, everybody," he called. "Be sure to pull the canoes up so they don't drift off. I'd hate to have to swim all the way back."

Mr. Jones helped Juliet out. Chili came bounding onto the sandbar and stood waiting. And then Juliet noticed a brown sack tucked back under her dad's seat.

"What's this?" she asked, reaching for it.

"I don't know," her father said. "It's not mine."

Chili looked at it. "Why don't you open it?"

"I'll let you do it, Dad." She handed the sack to him. "It probably belongs to somebody in one of the other canoes. Got mixed up somehow, I suppose."

While the other canoes unloaded, Juliet's father opened the brown bag. He reached inside. He took something out. And she saw his face change.

"What is it, Dad?" she asked.

"A compass."

At that moment Billy Rollins was walking by. "Let *me* see." He came over and exclaimed, "Why, that's *my* compass!"

Mr. Jones reached into the bag and pulled out something else. "That's my canteen!" Billy yelled.

Mr. Jones then took out a toothbrush, a knife, a barrette, two cups, and Joe's favorite hat. As he drew the articles out, one by one, everyone exclaimed and talked at the same time.

"That's my pocketknife!" Jack Tanner said.

Billy turned on Juliet. "It was in your canoe, wasn't it? You took those things, didn't you?"

"No, I didn't!" Juliet cried.

"I'll bet you did! Why else would they be in your canoe?"

"Now, Billy, calm down," Mr. Jones said. "Nobody knew who was going to ride in this canoe."

Mr. Harris, the leader of Juliet's group, reached for the bag. "I've never seen this bag before. Have any of you?"

A chorus of voices denied having seen it.

Mr. Harris put his hand into the sack and felt around.

"Anything else in there?" Juliet's dad asked.

"That's all—no, wait a minute."

When Mr. Harris's hand came out of the bag, it held a piece of paper.

"What's that?" Juliet asked.

"It looks like a note." Mr. Harris frowned. He unfolded the paper and read. Then he looked up. "It's for you, Juliet."

"For me?" Juliet took the paper. She stared at it and felt her face redden.

"What is it?"

"What does it say?"

"Read it, Juliet!"

Juliet read, "It says, 'Gotcha, Juliet! Didn't solve this one, did you?'"

"Is that all it says? Isn't it signed?" Joe cried.

"Yes, it's signed." Juliet slowly turned to face the one member of the crowd who wore a wide grin. "Chili Williams."

"Chili Williams, did *you* take all those things?" Flash asked.

"I sure did," Chili said, grinning even wider. "I wanted Juliet to have one mystery she couldn't solve."

A groan went up.

Mr. Jones said, "I'm afraid tricks that really upset other people aren't very nice, Chili."

"But it was just all in fun, Mr. Jones! Honest. I wasn't stealing anything. And everybody got their stuff back. Just one time I wanted 'Too Smart Jones' not to be so smart."

Juliet stood just looking at him.

Finally Chili said, "Are you mad at me, Juliet?"

"I already had it figured out. I already thought it must be you, Chili."

Billy hollered, "You didn't think any such thing! Nobody could have figured that out!"

Chili, however, did not laugh. "Did you really? That's hard to believe."

"I can prove it." Juliet fished her notebook out of her knapsack. "Jenny, read out loud the last thing I wrote in my journal. The very last entry."

Jenny opened the notebook. She began reading aloud. "'I'm pretty sure who has been taking things. What I can't figure out is *why* he would take them. He doesn't need that stuff. He isn't the kind of boy who would steal, either. So why did Chili do it? I'll have to ask him when we're alone at the end of the outing. I don't want anyone else to be mad at him for doing this. Maybe I can help him with his problem, whatever it is."

Jenny looked up, smiling. "That's all it says."

Suddenly Joe laughed. "Ha, Chili. And I'll bet you're responsible for the bear track and for the noises at night too. And you didn't fool my sister after all. She still got it all figured out. But how did you do it, Juliet?"

"It wasn't easy. I sort of noticed things he said . . . and where he was when certain things happened . . . and stuff like that."

Chili scratched his head with an embarrassed smile. "I give up," he said. "Too Smart Jones can figure out anything."

This was not, of course, the end of the matter. Juliet saw Mr. Williams take Chili off for a private conversation, and she was sure he was given a hard lecture.

When the lecture was over, Chili walked back and joined Juliet and the rest.

They all just looked at him.

"Well, Dad really gave it to me. He said I didn't have any business playing a trick like that. And I guess I didn't. So I'm sorry."

"Well, it *was* a little bit . . . frustrating for everybody, Chili," Juliet told him.

"*Frustrating?* I say his dad should have whomped him for it," Billy cried.

"Tell us how you did it," Joe said.

"Oh, that wasn't hard. I'd pick up something when nobody was looking. I'd put it in the bag, and then I'd stuff the bag in my backpack before anybody could see me."

Juliet did not want to scold Chili, for she liked him very much. But she thought she had to say, "I think I'd be careful if I were you before I did anything like that again."

"You can believe that," Chili said, sighing. "Never again."

"Anyway, nobody really lost anything. That part is good. And I got to solve another mystery, didn't I?"

Chili managed a laugh. Then he went to where Flash was sitting on the sand and gave him a high five. "No more practical jokes for me, Flash," he said.

"I think that's probably a good idea."

The homeward trip downriver was fun, but Juliet was glad when they got to their destination. The parents were waiting by the river with cars, and soon all were on their way home.

"You'll have to tell us all about it, Joe and Juliet," their mother said.

"We will, but it'll take a while," Joe said from the backseat.

Mrs. Jones looked around and smiled. "At least you didn't have to solve any mysteries, Juliet."

Juliet giggled. "How do you know that, Mom?"

"Because there couldn't be any mysteries to solve out in the middle of the woods."

Juliet grinned at her father in the rearview mirror, and he grinned back. Then they both grinned at Joe.

"I guess you're right, Mom. There are no more mysteries to solve out in the big woods."

Moody Press, a ministry of the Moody Bible Institute, is designed for education, evangelization, and edification. If we may assist you in knowing more about Christ and the Christian life, please write us without obligation:
Moody Press, c/o MLM, Chicago, IL 60610.

Get swept away in the many Gilbert Morris Adventures available from Moody Press:

"Too Smart" Jones

4025-8 Pool Party Thief
4026-6 Buried Jewels
4027-4 Disappearing Dogs
4028-2 Dangerous Woman
4029-0 Stranger in the Cave
4030-4 Cat's Secret
4031-2 Stolen Bicycles
4032-0 Wilderness Mystery
4033-9 Spooky Mansion
4034-7 Mysterious Artist

Come along for the adventures and mysteries Juliet "Too Smart" Jones always manages to find. She and her other homeschool friends solve these great adventures and learn biblical truths along the way. Ages 9-14

Seven Sleepers - The Lost Chronicles

3667-6 The Spell of the Crystal Chair
3668-4 The Savage Game of Lord Zarak
3669-2 The Strange Creatures of Dr. Korbo
3670-6 City of the Cyborgs
3671-4 The Temptations of Pleasure Island
3672-2 Victims of Nimbo
3673-0 The Terrible Beast of Zor

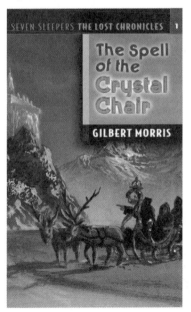

More exciting adventures from the Seven Sleepers. As these exciting young people attempt to faithfully follow Goél, they learn important moral and spiritual lessons. Come along with them as they encounter danger, intrigue, and mystery. Ages 10-14

MOODY
The Name You Can Trust
1-800-678-8812 www.MoodyPress.org

Seven Sleepers Series

Go with Josh and his friends as they are sent by Goél, their spiritual leader, on dangerous and challenging voyages to conquer the forces of darkness in the new world. Ages 10-14

Bonnets and Bugles Series

Follow good friends Leah Carter and Jeff Majors as they experience danger, intrigue, compassion, and love in these civil war adventures. Ages 10-14

MOODY
The Name You Can Trust
1-800-678-8812 www.MoodyPress.org